# TURNING THE TABLES

*Also by Rita Rudner*

*Tickled Pink: A Comic Novel*

*Rita Rudner's Guide to Men*

*Naked Beneath My Clothes*

*Rita Rudner*

# TURNING THE TABLES

*a novel*

Shaye Areheart Books
New York

Published in the United States by Shaye Areheart Books,
an imprint of the Crown Publishing Group, a division
of Random House, Inc., New York.
www.crownpublishing.com

Shaye Areheart Books and colophon are trademarks
of Random House, Inc.

Library of Congress Cataloging-in-Publication Data
Rudner, Rita.
Turning the tables : a novel / Rita Rudner.—1st ed.
1. Women executives—Fiction. 2. Casinos—Fiction.
3. Las Vegas (Nev.)—Fiction. I. Title.
PS3568.U3335T87  2006
813'.54—dc22                               2006011312

ISBN-10: 0-307-33912-2
ISBN-13: 978-0-307-33912-6

Printed in the United States of America

DESIGN BY ELINA D. NUDELMAN

10 9 8 7 6 5 4 3 2 1

First Edition

For our dog, Bonkers,
for sitting under the desk and never having
any opinions.

**ACKNOWLEDGMENTS**

*Thanks to the city of Las Vegas
for being so silly and so good to me.*

# TURNING THE TABLES

# PROLOGUE

It was a little after midnight when Christian Sacco received a phone call from Heaven.

"It's me," said a disembodied voice. "I need you back in the office. Now."

"Sure. What's the problem?"

"Not on the phone. Just get here."

Although president of the largest casino in Las Vegas, Richard Summerford was very much a nine-to-five guy and a call to one of his employees after hours was an unusual occurrence. Christian drove hurriedly along the Las Vegas Strip to Heaven, anxious to discover why as director of entertainment he had been summoned back to work. When he entered Summerford's office, Jimmy Falanucci, the head of security, was already there.

"What's up, Boss?" Christian asked. He never called Summerford "Boss" unless he was attempting maximum ingratiation.

"Show him," a terse Summerford ordered Jimmy.

"This is from the cage three hours ago," Jimmy explained, slipping a DVD into a player and pressing "play."

The flat-screen television in Richard's office flickered on. Footage from four surveillance cameras covering the casino cage began to roll. Christian studied each quadrant carefully.

"Hey, that's Allie," said Christian, pointing to the bottom-right corner of the screen. "We had lunch today."

"She's cashing out chips," Richard explained abruptly. "Twenty one-thousand-dollar chips. They're counterfeit."

Nobody spoke.

"I'm sure there's a logical explanation," Christian finally stammered. "Allie would never . . ."

"I had her office searched ten minutes ago," Summerford interrupted. "We found these hidden behind a bookshelf."

Standing up, Richard emptied a bag of over a hundred counterfeit chips onto his desk.

"Oh, Jesus . . . ," whispered Christian.

"I've had her detained by Security," Summerford continued.

"Look, I know Allie. If she is involved in this, then somebody put her up to it," Christian protested, breaking in. "Let me talk to her, Richard. I'll get the whole story."

Richard Summerford looked irritated.

"Please, Boss, as a favor to me," Christian pushed.

"We'll interview her together," Richard said finally.

A few minutes later, a burly security guard escorted Allie Bowen to a bare, airless interview room in the bowels of the building.

"What the hell is going on?" Allie demanded, stumbling awkwardly into the room. "Get me Mr. Summerford. Now."

The security guard said nothing, and just stood by the door to bar her possible exit. Allie refused to sit. She paced impatiently, feeling both her antiperspirant and her self-confidence beginning to falter. The minutes crawled by until, finally, Christian and Summerford entered the room. Allie looked relieved.

"Richard . . . Christian . . . there's been some sort of screwup. This is outrageous. Tell him to release me immediately," Allie demanded, gesturing toward the guard.

Her voice sounded confident, but her trembling top lip betrayed her fragile emotional state.

"Turn off the surveillance cameras," Summerford barked. "I don't want this recorded. Sit down, Allie."

Summerford's hostile tone made Allie blanch. She wilted into the chair as the security guard turned off the camera. Summerford emphatically dumped the counterfeit chips onto the table and turned inquiringly toward Allie. "Recognize these?"

Allie looked surprised. "What? No. Why?" she stammered.

"We found these hidden in your office."

"That's impossible," she insisted.

"Is it?" said Summerford. He contemplatively rubbed his tongue side to side across his top lip as he decided how next to proceed. "Will you empty your handbag, please?"

Allie laughed inappropriately. "My handbag? Why?"

Her voice sounded hollow and thin as it resonated around the bare room.

"Just do it, Allie," Christian implored. "This is all probably just a stupid misunderstanding."

Allie shrugged and emptied the contents of her handbag onto the bare desk in front of her. Summerford picked up the roll of hundred-dollar bills that had fallen out.

"What's this?"

"That's the money I changed for a high roller," Allie babbled. "For Christian. I did it for Christian."

Christian reached for the table to steady himself. "What?" he asked disbelievingly.

"What's she talking about?" Summerford asked, looking hard at Christian.

"I have absolutely no idea," Christian replied, looking dumbfounded.

Allie felt both the room and her stomach shrink as she suddenly realized just how swiftly a life can unravel. The tears that had been threatening to course down her cheeks finally began their journey.

"I want a lawyer," she sobbed.

# ONE

Six months earlier, before being accused of forgery by an officer of one of America's biggest companies, Allie

Bowen lay blissfully in the arms of Christian Sacco, the man she had been with since her separation from her husband . . . and, truth be told, a little before that as well. The shrill ring of the phone woke them both.

"Stay asleep," Allie whispered. "It's probably for me."

Even though Christian Sacco was the third most important executive within the casino hierarchy, it was Allie's job as Heaven's vice president of marketing and public relations that was more likely to generate a middle-of-the-night phone call.

"Allie Bowen," she said sleepily.

"It's Falanucci. We've got a Code Yellow. NBC news is already here."

"I'll be there in ten minutes," she said, reaching for her pants.

"What is it? What's happened?" asked Christian, as Allie dressed hurriedly.

"There's been a Code Yellow."

"A Code Yellow? A jumper?"

"Uh-huh."

"It wasn't that bastard pianist in the cocktail lounge, was it?" asked Christian hopefully.

"I don't think so," said Allie, who smiled as she buttoned her blouse.

"Shame."

Allie bent down and gave Christian a soft kiss.

"See you at work, darling," she said.

*Teasingly, from the* Las Vegas Strip, a passerby can only vaguely discern the giant, blurry outline of Heaven's facade. The city's most impressive monument is deliberately hidden twenty-four hours a day behind an obscuring cumulous mountain of man-made fog.

The only way to see more clearly is to approach more closely. Every day tens of thousands make the decision to do just that by stepping onto the walkway that moves in only one direction. As the people-mover pierces the fog, first-time visitors invariably let out an audible gasp. Heads turn upward and mouths gape open in wonder. Visiting eyes follow the intricate, ornate carving of the front facade, full of trumpeting angels and Dale Chihuly–designed stained-glass windows, as it soars skyward.

Sammy Kirvin, Heaven's octogenarian primary stockholder, came up with the paradise theme himself. Ancient Rome, New York, England, Paris, and Egypt were already well represented on Las Vegas Boulevard. Sammy cursed the fact that all the good countries were gone. Holland had tulips and cumbersome shoes, but that was not enough on which to hang a multibillion-dollar hotel. Afghanistan had caves, which was tempting, but of questionable taste given the current state of geopolitics. Russia had been seriously considered. Sammy liked that one; if something went wrong, such as room service failing to show up, it could just be passed off as part of the theme. However, the more conservative members of his board had vetoed that suggestion.

Brainstorming session followed brainstorming session, until the night Sammy Kirvin experienced a thematic epiphany. In flowerier interviews, he liked to suggest that maybe God himself had chosen to imbue him with the idea. After all, God had always liked the desert. He'd set the Bible there.

Built over four years at a cost of three billion dollars, Heaven is quite simply and without reservation the most spectacular architectural achievement of the early twenty-first century. Stepping off the moving walkway, gawking visitors continue forward through St. Peter's Gates and into the interior where a team of St. Peters—actually, trained security guards with concealed Glocks beneath their wings—welcome each gambler with a flutter and a frisk.

Beyond the guards, the atrium ascends to a roof whose trompe l'oeil effect of absolute perspective makes it appear as though one is still outside and staring up into the cosmos. Wrapped around the circumference of the casino floor are 9,750 rooms, making Heaven the largest hotel in the world. It is also the most profitable.

Leaving her car in Heaven's executive parking lot, Allie bounded up the escalator directly into the lobby. The first thing she saw was the camera crew from the local NBC affiliate. Rikki Green, the ambitious reporter who caught the story, had cornered a blood-spattered hotel guest.

"What exactly did you see, Mr. Beechnut?" Rikki was purring, pointing her microphone toward Mr. Beechnut's unfortunately decorated face.

"I turned around just as the fat man exploded on the carpet."

"How did you feel?" Rikki pressed. "What were you thinking? Did you panic?"

"Panic? No, I didn't have time to panic. I just opened my mouth to scream and—"

Rikki interrupted, excitedly. "Did you swallow anything?"

"Oh my God, I don't know. I was covered in . . . whatever this is," he moaned, picking gelatinous bits from his jacket. "What if I swallowed something? What if my boy swallowed something?"

Rikki lowered her microphone down to little Augie Beechnut's mouth. "How old are you, dear?"

"Eight," the little boy replied.

"Can you tell me what you saw?"

"I saw his insides explode and everything," Augie enthused. "It completely rocked."

Allie was too far away to hear what was being said, but the triumphant look on Rikki Green's face was enough. At a dead run, Allie lunged at the microphone, pushing it to one side and positioning herself between the camera and the Beechnuts.

"Hello," she panted at the Beechnuts. "On behalf of everyone here at Heaven, I would like to extend our most sincere apologies. We're so sorry you had to witness this tragedy. If you'll just give me one minute, I'll help you get settled."

Though they looked rather stunned at the breathless intrusion, Mom, Dad, and Augie agreeably shuffled to one side. Allie turned to Rikki Green.

"Rikki," she said sweetly, "don't make a bad situation even worse. Think of that poor family and the family of the deceased."

"No can do, Allie. This is a big story," Rikki said. "Great visuals."

Allie swallowed hard. "Great visuals." This was not good.

"Please, Rikki," Allie cajoled. "I'll owe you big-time. Christian has Cher coming into the arena at the end of the month. I'll get you front-row seats."

Rikki crooked an eyebrow. She knew the owner of her station was close friends with many members of Heaven's board of directors. One call to her employer and the story would in all probability be scotched anyway. At least this way she would get an up-close look at what was really going on with Cher's face.

"Fine," she said. "You owe me, Allie."

Allie hurried over to Jimmy Falanucci, the casino's director of security, who was busy coordinating the cleaning crew's operation.

"Where the hell are Richard and Frank?" she asked, referring to the president and vice president of Heaven respectively.

"On a plane coming back from some seminar bullshit in New York. Someone's trying to get hold of 'em."

"What do we know about the jumper?" Allie asked, eyeing the gruesome leftovers.

"Mr. Average from Ohio. We're helping the cops piece together his evening from the tapes. Started out betting ten bucks a hand and ended up a hundred thousand in the hole. Somehow got up to the top floor. Jumped. Burst."

"What about the family that got splattered?"

"The Beechnuts. From Illinois. Flew in tonight."

"OK, thanks, Jimmy," she said. Taking a deep breath, Allie made her way over to the Beechnuts.

"On behalf of everyone here at the casino," she said, using her most placating tone, "let me formally apologize for this unfortunate incident."

"Who are you?" asked a confused Mrs. Beechnut.

Allie proffered her card to each Beechnut. "Allie Bowen. I work here at Heaven. Let me begin by promising you that your entire visit to Heaven will be comped. I've had you upgraded to one of our luxury suites. If there's anything you need while you're here—absolutely anything—you just call me."

Placated by the promise of free shows and free food, the Beechnuts headed up to their room to shower off the remains of Mr. Average from Ohio. Some hours later Allie received a summons to Richard Summerford's office.

"You handled this incident very well, Allie," Summerford announced with a smile. "The Beechnuts have already signed a legal waiver exonerating us from any blame."

Allie blinked. *Legal waiver?* "Ummm," she said. "Great."

"I'm grateful, and I'll make sure the board knows what a good job you did. About time we had a few more women in upper management."

*More women?* thought Allie. *How about just one?*

"Thank you, Mr. Summerford," she said, then stood, smiled, and left, anxious to tell Christian about her success.

# TWO

Magician Barry Houdini glanced at the watch his ex-wife had bought him for his thirtieth birthday from one of the jewelry stores in the Forum Shops at Caesars Palace. It said 1:45, but the watch had been running slow ever since he accidentally dropped it into a bowl of goldfish during a trick. Barry knew he should get it fixed, but it was easier to add a few extra minutes mentally, and Barry was an easygoing kind of guy. That was why his wife had fallen in love with him. It was also why she had left him.

Glancing again at the watch, Barry calculated that it was really one fiftyish. As the Barry Houdini afternoon show of mystical, magical illusion (includes one free watered-down drink) supposedly began at two but in reality never started until ten after, Barry figured he still had time to grab a beer at the bar.

Wait a second, he thought. This was Sunday, right? Wasn't he supposed to do something on Sunday? Yes. Yes, he was. Damn. He was supposed to turn his watch back an hour. So, he was actually an hour early for his show. He could have slept an extra sixty minutes. Damn, again.

The Pinwheel Casino was located in the downiest bit of downtown. Most of its clientele sported a variety of physical oddities: a mangled foot, a missing finger, a lazy eye. The attraction of downtown was its cheaper prices, lower minimum bets, and better odds. It had none of the bells and whistles of the Strip experience, but for the real Vegas aficionado that was its charm.

Finishing his beer, Barry headed toward the glorified lounge the Pinwheel described as its Broadway Theatre, home of THE WORLD'S GREATEST AFTERNOON MAGIC SHOW STARRING BARRY HOUDINI. He noticed with surprise that the area where people usually milled and smoked was empty. Granted, the 102-seat theater was never packed, but it was never empty, either. Strange. Barry looked again at his watch. It was 3:10, which meant it was actually 2:05.

Through the ambient casino hum, Barry heard a familiar jingling approaching fast on his left. Kenny Hess, manager of the Broadway Theatre, was famous for the number of keys he sported on the left side of his jeans' belt loop. The keys forced Kenny to slope to one side, resulting in the exposure of a portion of hairy Kenny midriff in between T-shirt and jeans that was more of Kenny than anyone really wanted to see.

"Where the hell were you?" Kenny demanded.

"What do you mean, dude? I'm here."

"It's four ten," Kenny scolded. "Your lousy show was supposed to be at two o'clock."

Barry looked at his watch and shook his head. "It's two ten. Your watch is wrong."

Kenny sighed. "Barry, I don't believe this. Didn't you turn your watch ahead an hour last night?"

"Ahead? Wait a minute. It's spring, isn't it? 'Spring back, fall forward.'"

"No, you dummy. It's 'spring forward, fall back.'"

"Dude, you're wrong. I spring back and then I fall forward."

"No," an impatient Kenny insisted. "You're wrong. You're always wrong."

Barry pondered, and inwardly admitted there was a distinct possibility that Kenny was correct. "Man, I'm so sorry. It will not happen again."

"You're right it won't happen again. You're fired."

Barry recoiled. "Dude, that's cold. It was an honest mistake. Look, I'm turning my watch forward right now."

Barry removed his watch and began to twiddle it. "I'm springing forward. I'm even making it a little fast. See, four fifteen. Four twenty. I'll go to four twenty-two. I'll never be late again."

Kenny's tone became a little more conciliatory. Barry was a nice guy. "If things were really happening for you here, it would be a different story," he reasoned. "But you're only averaging fifty people an afternoon and most of them are comped. It's coming from the top. I've gotta get more bodies in here."

Barry had been fired before but, as in falling in love, each time is like the first.

"I'll get my birds now," he said dejectedly. "I'll get the rest of the magic boxes tomorrow. Will you tell Wanda?"

Barry didn't want to be the one to break it to the world's

oldest magician's assistant that she was out of a job. She had a sick mother and a bad back. Barry had to intentionally slow down the "sticking the knives through the box" trick to give her time to bend down.

"Sure. I'll find her a job here somewhere . . . something behind the bar. It's time she got offstage. I can tell you now . . . there have been complaints. I've seen barstools with better legs." Kenny extended a conciliatory hand and then jangled away.

Back in his rented apartment, Barry sipped on a beer and stared morosely at the Jackson Three—Michael, Jermaine, and Tito—the now-unemployed avian costars of Barry's show. Originally, of course, there had been five birds and the Jackson reference had made a lot more sense. Tragically, two birds had died of heart attacks after being caught in Barry's sleeve during a trick. That had been a bad show. The Jackson Three were usually happy show birds. Now they huddled in a corner of their cage, their little parakeet heads hanging low as they blinked despondently in the direction of their bird-father. Slumped on his sofa, Barry cracked open another beer and pondered his life. Now what?

His ex-wife warned him this day would come. "You live in never-never land," she had insisted.

"No I don't," Barry had countered. "I live on Sahara and Decatur."

"You're just the sort of person who ends up broke and homeless. Get it together. Grow up."

Okay. Fine. Maybe he did smoke the more than occasional joint and maybe he did almost set the apartment on fire when he accidentally fused that hot frying pan onto the kitchen counter. The pan was still there. Barry had never bothered to pry it off. He thought it looked kinda cool. But could he really end up broke and homeless? Exhaling deeply, he picked up the phone that might soon be cut off and dialed someone who might be able to help.

The last voice Allie expected to hear when she picked up the phone was that of Barry Houdini, her ex-husband. She was stunned. She wasn't surprised that Barry was unemployed; indeed, she was impressed that he had kept the Pinwheel gig as long as he had. No, what surprised Allie was that Barry had turned to her for help, especially after their last conversation.

"Barry, you need to make tapes," Allie had advised. "You need to buy new costumes. Invent new tricks. Improve and move up. Don't you have any ambition?"

Barry stopped rolling his breakfast joint and considered.

"No," he decided, then continued rolling.

"You're thirty. Don't you have plans?"

"Yes, I do. I have plans."

"Like what?"

"Well . . . I plan to watch Regis and Kelly in five minutes if you stop talking."

With sad resignation, Allie had packed a bag and moved out, her hopes and dreams for her husband's career finally dashed. She hadn't seen Barry since.

Now, Allie wanted to help. She knew she would feel less guilty about how happy she was in her new job and her new relationship if she could somehow assist Barry in his life. They had, after all, had some very good times together.

Allie knew there was a singer in Heaven's recently

remodeled Seraphim Lounge who quite simply needed to go. She had heard someone actually tip a waiter to turn down this singer's microphone. Maybe Christian could be persuaded to replace her with Barry?

Later that same evening, while waiting for her tardy boyfriend, Allie ordered another cosmopolitan and began to analyze what benefits Barry brought to the table. Surely, Christian had to be thinking of firing that dreadful lounge singer. Allie was amazed he had hired her in the first place. As a replacement, Barry would be a fast-and-cheap alternative.

Also, Christian's birthday was approaching. Though he had been dropping hints, he was being uncharacteristically reticent about what it was, specifically, that he wanted. Perhaps she could work that. "If I give him what he wants," she reasoned, "he'll be more inclined to give me what I want." Smiling to herself, Allie looked up to see Christian gliding toward the table.

"Hi, good-looking," Christian whispered as he kissed her on the cheek. "What's that smile for?"

"It's nothing. I'll tell you later. Have a drink. Tell me how your day was."

"Fucking has-been lounge singer can just eat shit and die," he griped.

Allie's jaw dropped. This was too good to be true. Was he having a fight with that shabby chanteuse already?

"She is bad," Allie concurred.

"What? Not 'her,' 'him.' That asswipe I booked into the Galaxy Theater tonight. He wants all his money up front or he doesn't perform. I had to go to the cage and draw him thirty grand in cash. Who were *you* talking about?"

"Malfi Molini in the Seraphim Lounge."

"What's wrong with Malfi?" Christian asked as he reached for some bread.

"What's wrong with her? She's tone-deaf. She's holding notes that don't exist," said Allie, passing the butter.

"Hey, she's a beautiful woman. People don't come just to hear her sing. They come to ogle. It's an experience."

"Yes, but it's a bad experience. We're the top hotel on the Strip. We shouldn't be featuring a no-talent bimbo like her."

Christian froze. "Wait a fucking second. When did you become a talent scout?" he snarled.

Christian was always perfectly manicured and possessed an apparently endless supply of five-thousand-dollar European suits. Indeed, Allie had often wondered how Christian managed to afford his extravagant lifestyle choices on an entertainment director's salary. But Christian was a child of the streets of South Philly. His humble background only became exposed when he opened his mouth; his colorful language and grammar revealing the tough street kid that seethed below the sparkling surface.

Clearly, this was not a good time for her to fish for a new job for her ex-husband. Allie decided to retreat and rethink her strategy about how to manipulate Christian into doing what she wanted.

Later, when they had finished dinner and returned to Christian's house, Allie slipped on her sheerest, shortest, laciest teddy. Christian was already in bed, flicking through the television channels as if he were in a flicking race. Allie wondered how he could even know what he was watching before he flicked onto another station. She glided into bed beside Christian and snuggled against his chest.

"Sweetheart," she cooed. "About your birthday present . . . what exactly is it that you want?"

Christian looked carefully at Allie and equivocated. "I don't think you'd be into it."

"Into what? Tell me."

"Well, it's something I've always wanted to try and it would just be for my birthday."

"A car? A food? What?"

Christian took a deep breath, turned off the TV, then forged ahead. "There's a convention in town next week—"

Allie interrupted. "I know; the motorcycle convention. You want a Harley?"

"No, not that convention, there's another one. It's kind of a swingers' thing."

Allie's eyes opened wide. "'A swingers' thing'?" she stammered. "You want me to have sex with another couple?"

"It's not like that. It's called Sybaris and it's really classy. There's caviar, champagne, condoms, and all top-quality people. It's really fun."

Allie looked at Christian suspiciously. "I thought you'd never tried it before?"

"Only once. Cassandra and I went last year. We had a blast."

*Oh, great,* Allie thought. Cassandra was Christian's gorgeous, five-foot-ten ex-girlfriend who was a showgirl in *Jubilee!* at Bally's.

"Can I think about it?" she asked, unwilling to be

trumped by Cassandra but terrified of actually agreeing to go.

"No problem. This thing is always sold out, so I'll have Jane and Bill reserve us tickets just in case."

"Jane and Bill?" Allie asked. "Aren't those very straight names for people who organize swingers' parties?"

"Those aren't their real names, dear," Christian replied, unfastening her lingerie.

# THREE

Allie surveyed the couples filing into the Sybaris event as she found herself once again waiting for her unpunctual paramour. Although the weather outside was warm, most of the women wore coats. Allie caught glimpses here and there of the outfits on offer underneath, and even though she had carefully picked out the tightest and shortest dress she owned, she could see she was not even in the sexual ballpark. As she considered the possibility of buying a pair of scissors and cutting holes in her outfit, Christian waltzed up with a mischievous grin on his face and an anticipatory spring in his step. He was only five minutes late. This must be a good party.

"Do I look okay?" he asked, twirling around.

"You look great. How 'bout me?" Allie struck a pose.

Christian stepped back and surveyed his girlfriend.

"Sure. I like it. It's demure. I already have our name-tags; you're Serena and I'm Marlon."

"OK," Allie replied hesitantly.

Arm in arm, they strolled into the ballroom. Drapes separated the different areas of the room into smaller, more intimate spaces. Some contained sofas, some beds, and some dance floors. Wherever Allie looked there were people engaged in, well, if not sexual activity, then certainly presexual activity. Most of the women were overly tanned, overly teased, and overly breasted. While the men were dressed mostly in suits, the women's bodies were more on display than the plastic desserts outside a mid-priced Italian restaurant.

Unsure of herself, Allie held tightly to Christian's arm and asked, "OK, so what do we do now?"

"We mingle," advised Christian, scanning the crowd. "If we see anyone we find attractive, we take it from there. Come on, beautiful, let's see who's here."

They were quickly approached by a statuesque blonde in a bra that covered everything except her nipples.

"Hello," she purred. "I'm Natasha. Would you like to lick my nipples?"

"No, thank you," Allie replied primly.

Christian, however, seemed to think it was a good idea and lurched forward. As they fell into the sofa, Natasha's hand slipped down Christian's pants. After thirty seconds or so, it was over.

"That's enough," Natasha pronounced, and then walked away.

Christian straightened his clothing. "That was fantastic," he exclaimed, eyes glistening. "See? You just have to be open-minded. She had fun. I had fun. Nobody got hurt."

Allie did not look convinced.

"Look, I'll get you a drink," Christian suggested. "Just hold tight."

"OK," she said, smiling tentatively but thinking, *Try not to lick anyone on your way to the bar.*

As she sat down on an empty sofa, a couple immediately plopped down next to her. They looked even straighter than she did. The woman wore no makeup and a loose-fitting, black dress. She even sported streaks of gray in her curly black hair, which, after the sea of Crayola heads she'd been witnessing, Allie actually found refreshing. The man was equally nondescript and appeared to have come straight from the office. He even carried a briefcase.

"Hello," Allie said. "I'm Allie. I mean Selina. No, Serena."

"We're the Slaughsons, from Maine. I've never seen anything like this before, have you?"

"No. It's pretty wild."

"I think it's disgraceful," commented the woman.

"It is unusual," Allie said, wondering if this couple had mistakenly wandered into the wrong convention.

"All these people fondling each other in public," the woman clucked with disapproval. Her face suddenly lit up. "Have you tried electric clamps?"

As Mr. Slaughson opened his briefcase to reveal several metal contraptions, Allie jumped up quickly from the sofa.

"You know, I've got to be over there," Allie said, unable to think of an appropriate exit line, but dearly wanting to move away from the clamps.

"They're not labial," the woman quickly added.

"In that case, I'm not interested," Allie falsely protested. "It's labial or nothing for me!"

The clamp woman stared in disbelief.

"I can make them labial, it's only a small adjustment," she offered.

"No, it's too late," Allie retorted, backing away. "Not labial? That's just absurd. Why even bother clamping?"

Free of the Slaughsons, Allie searched for Christian, which was like hunting for a needle in a fuckstack. After five minutes she found him surveying an intertwined female threesome with the concentration of an Olympic judge. He was not alone. Standing beside him, wearing a shimmering deep gray bodysuit, a rhinestone-studded collar, and a leash, was a towering Amazon bearing a striking resemblance to a Great Dane. It was Cassandra.

"Look who I found," Christian announced brightly, handing Allie her drink.

"Hi, Cassandra," Allie murmured unenthusiastically.

"Woof," Cassandra replied.

"Cassie is very into the dog thing tonight. Watch what happens if I scratch her belly."

Allie smiled, thinking, *Do I have to? And did he have to call her Cassie?*

Christian scratched Cassandra's belly and her leg began to twitch.

Allie smiled again. "That's nice," she said weakly.

Bizarrely, Cassandra began to lick Allie's face.

"She likes you," commented Christian. "I like you, too. What d'ya say?"

"I don't know . . . 'Thank you'?" Allie cautiously replied.

"No, you know . . ."

Christian gestured toward the threesome in front of them, hoping a visual aid would help Allie grasp what he was getting at. It did.

"You've got to be kidding me."

Cassandra began to whimper.

"Wait here, Cassie. I need to talk to Allie alone."

Christian pulled Allie to one side.

"You've hurt her feelings now," Christian pouted. "Don't you want to have some fun?"

"You said I didn't have to do anything I didn't want to do."

"And you don't, but she's really putting herself out there. C'mon, what d'ya say? This is my birthday present, after all."

Allie and Christian looked over at Cassandra. The showgirl's head tilted sadly to one side as her tongue lolled out of the side of her mouth.

"What do you want me to do? Offer her a treat?"

Annoyed, he said, "I'll just go upstairs with Cassandra then."

"Christian, that was not our deal," Allie replied firmly.

"I said *you* didn't have to do anything you didn't want

to. I didn't say I wasn't going to do anything you didn't want me to do. C'mon, Allie, that's what these parties are for. Once a year you indulge in a fantasy."

Allie knew Christian's logic was self-serving, but she also knew that if she maintained her position, her boyfriend would soon be in bed with his ex-girlfriend, athletically exploring a variety of canine positions.

*If I go upstairs, I can at least control what happens,* Allie rationalized inwardly.

"OK, I'll try it," she announced outwardly.

Christian turned back to Cassandra and took hold of her leash.

"Come on, girl."

Upstairs, when Christian opened the door, Allie's eyes quickly scanned the multibedroomed suite, expecting to see an abundance of copulation. She saw nothing. The fantasies were taking place in separate bedrooms behind closed doors. DO NOT DISTURB signs hung from every knob.

"Cassandra," Christian commanded. "Go scratch on somebody's door like you did last year."

"Wait. You've done this dog thing before?" asked Allie, now growing suspicious.

"Just once. Last year."

It was all starting to fit together, like a particularly complicated game of naked Twister. Allie was beginning to suspect that she was just a pawn in Christian's game of sexual chess. He'd probably been fantasizing about this all year.

Just then, the door to one of the bedrooms swung open and two women wearing scanty underwear and handcuffs were pushed through it by a policeman.

"Oh my God, Christian, they're raiding the place," Allie exclaimed.

"Hi, how ya' doin'?" the policeman said casually, nodding to Christian. "The room's all yours. Don't worry about the mess in the bathroom. It's fake blood."

Once in the room, Cassandra began to pull on her leash, quickly throwing Christian down on the bed and trapping him from above on all fours. Loosening his tie with her hands and pulling it off with her teeth, she began undressing him.

Enraged, Allie tapped Cassandra on the shoulder.

"Excuse me, Rover. My turn."

Growling, Cassandra lowered her head and with one swift move clamped her teeth down on the side of Allie's neck.

"Ow! Jesus. You're a frigging nutcase," Allie shrieked in surprise. "Christian, she bit me. Your crazy ex-girlfriend just bit me." Allie touched her hand to her neck and stared at the drop of blood on her fingers. "I'm bleeding!"

"Only a little. Don't overreact," Christian whined; things were not going as he had planned.

Allie jumped up, her hand still clamped to her neck. "OK, you two can continue on with this freak show. I'm going back to the real world where people sleep together either because they care about each other or for money."

Allie's eyes began to well up with tears as she pressed a Kleenex to her neck.

Cassandra metamorphosed back into a human being. "Hey, Allie, I'm sorry. I just got a little carried away. I didn't really mean to bite you."

"You're kidding, right?" Allie asked angrily, waving a bloodstained tissue at Cassie. "How do you explain this? Christian, I'm going home. Are you coming with me?"

"Chris, you might as well go," Cassandra advised. "My whole dog thing is blown. I can't just turn it on. It takes hours of preparation."

"Well, this little fantasy's sure shot," Christian said angrily, straightening his clothing. Allie took a step toward Christian, tears streaming down her face.

"I'm sorry, I just don't get it. I don't begin to get it," Allie began to hiccup. "Christian, I thought you cared about me."

"Why can't you get it? It's not about fucking caring about you," Christian snarled. "It's about pretending and acting a little crazy once a year."

Cassandra stood up, saying, "Look, why don't you two go home and work things out? I'm sure there are people out there waiting to use this room for something other than couple's therapy. Allie, I'm sorry. Christian told me you'd be into it. And don't worry, I've had all my shots. Anyway, I think you've stopped bleeding."

With that, a two-legged Cassandra blew Christian a kiss and pranced out the door. Allie and Christian remained in the room and stared at each other in icy silence. Allie glanced at her watch; it was 12:30. Discussions about relationships never go well after midnight.

Christian was furious. As far as he was concerned, tonight had been a test and Allie had failed miserably. It was time to cut bait. "Allie, I think you should move out," he announced coldly.

Allie was stunned. Before she could respond, he had

crossed to the door. He looked back. "You need to get your stuff out of my house. Tonight," he said. Then he turned and left.

Allie slumped onto the bed and burst into tears. That was it? She'd abandoned her marriage for this man and this was how he was going to end it?

Just then, she heard a knock on the door. Turning, she began to apologize.

"Christian, I didn't mean to ruin . . ."

But it wasn't Christian. It was two men dressed in black leather masks and matching briefs.

"Are you finished in here?" asked one of the men. "Because if you're not, you're welcome to join us."

Allie screamed. She could not believe this was happening. She stumbled out of the room and down to the lobby to catch a taxi. She was going home. To pack.

# FOUR

Christian had initially been attracted to sensible, midwestern Allie because he felt she could be a career asset. Most of the upper echelon of Heaven's executives had wives like her: blonde, toned, white-toothed, and bubbly.

Christian had felt the relationship could help him fulfill his ultimate ambition of acquiring Richard Summerford's job, seven-figure salary, and stock options.

The reality of Allie had, however, driven him crazy. She represented Christian's first serious attempt at living with someone, and Christian had come to realize it wasn't for him. He rationalized that Hugh Hefner had tried marriage and hadn't been able to do it, either. Some men were simply psychologically unsuited to monogamy. Christian wasn't a failure. He was a Hefner.

Knowing that Allie was probably at his place, packing, Christian decided to drive to Heaven instead. As he drove, he considered the joy of no more shoes found in strange places, no more half-eaten yogurts in the refrigerator, and no more tiny female thongs finding their way into his precisely arranged sock drawer. He concocted a mental balance sheet and concluded he was in relationship profit. So, he reasoned, was Allie. Her relationship with him had helped her career within the company and clearly had been the impetus of the demise of her marriage to that loser magician. If Christian had been selfish, he could have strung Allie along for all of her good years—certainly the rest of her twenties—and then ended it when she passed her peak. This way, she was still hot enough to snag a suitably wealthy and connected husband. Yes, as he saw it, Allie owed him a big, fat thank-you.

After snaking his way through the Saturday night Strip traffic, Christian parked his leased Mercedes SL550 in Heaven's executive car park and entered the casino through a connecting walkway. He was gratified to see a full house emerging from the midnight performance of the casino's signature entertainment attraction, Gravitas. Assembled at a cost of over two hundred million dollars, Gravitas had been created by a former member of Cirque du Soleil's management team. The gimmick of Gravitas was that the theater appeared entirely weightless. Using technology developed by NASA to train astronauts, audience members were suspended around the top of the room, the show happening beneath them. Every performance had been sold out since opening night. Two years into its run, Gravitas was still the undisputed number one must-see show on the Strip.

Christian noticed that the crowds pressing around the gaming tables were in some instances six to eight people thick and all the slot machines appeared occupied. A thick pall of tobacco smoke hung in the air despite the best efforts of the state-of-the-art air-recycling apparatus that completely regenerated the casino's air every twenty minutes in an attempt to help people stay awake and therefore gamble longer.

As Christian moved through the gaming area, he spotted one of the pit bosses, Angelo Salero, beckon to him.

"Your friend Max Lohmann ain't doing too well tonight," Angelo announced, gesturing toward a roulette table in the high-roller lounge.

Christian looked across the casino floor and waved to Malfi, Max's girlfriend, who, standing by her losing beau's side, looked as though she were burying a child every time Max lost another potential Versace outfit on the spin of the wheel.

"How much has he lost?" Christian asked.

"About a hundred K," said Angelo.

Christian shrugged. The amount would hurt, but he had no doubt Max could afford it.

Christian had been introduced to Max Lohmann just over nine months ago by Bill Silverman, the casino's head of player development. Silverman had felt that Lohmann was a medium roller capable of graduating to high-roller status with a little assistance. Christian's assistance.

"He's schtupping this local girl, see?" Bill had said. "A singer. I thought maybe you could do something for her. You know . . . so he'll spend more time at the tables."

Christian had invited Max for a drink and listened to his story. Lohmann owned a highly successful plastics business in Los Angeles and a highly expensive house in Brentwood containing an enormously expensive wife and an outrageously expensive teenage daughter. Over recent years, occasional overnight and weekend trips to Vegas had proven a welcome respite for Max from both the business and the family, especially when he had hooked up with Malfi, a sexy cocktail waitress at Caesars Palace.

At Max's behest, Christian went to hear Malfi sing in a bar in Henderson. She believed she was the next Mariah Carey. Christian decided she had more chance of being the next Jim Carrey. However, he sensed an opportunity to supplement his overstretched salary.

"Well, kid, what d'you think?" Max asked him eagerly. "She's busting my balls about getting her a job. Can you do anything for her? She sings great, doesn't she?"

"She's unusual," said Christian diplomatically.

"Tell you what . . . I'll gamble exclusively in Heaven if you give her a job," offered Max.

"It's not that simple," Christian parried. "You know how Vegas works."

"Sure I do. I also know I blew almost a million dollars in this fucking town last year. Having my business exclusively is a good deal. Look, kid, this girl's the best thing that's happened to me for years. She's only twenty fucking three . . . can you believe that? But I'm not a patsy. I won't be ripped off. If you don't want to help me, I'll go someplace where they'll appreciate my business. Another way of looking at this is I'm doing you a favor, given how talented she is."

Christian smiled tensely. *She wouldn't get past the audition for the audition for* American Idol, *you fat, horny fuck,* he thought.

Out loud, Christian said, "I'd like to help. The singer in the Seraphim Lounge has a two-year contract. I'd have to buy that out. Then there's another act who's been promised first right of refusal."

None of this was true. The current attraction in the Seraphim Lounge had actually been made a better offer by the Rio and was leaving in six weeks. Max's timing could not have been better, but Christian was going to squeeze the most out of Max's wallet that he could.

"How much?" asked Max, cutting to the chase. "I won't be ripped off. Bill Silverman said you were a reasonable fella."

"Let me ask you a somewhat delicate question," Christian began. "Do you pay Malfi an allowance?"

"Two grand a week," the middle-aged businessman quickly replied. "She needs some moving-around money."

"OK. I'll pay Malfi three thousand a week to sing in the Seraphim Lounge."

"What's the catch?"

"You're going to pay me the two grand you were paying her. It won't be for me, you understand," lied Christian. "I'll use it to smooth away any wrinkles. Make some contracts go away."

Max extended a pudgy, hairy hand. "Bill Silverman was right about you," he said with a wink. "You're a reasonable fella."

# FIVE

Bereft and miserable, Allie spent Saturday night in a shabby motel near the Stratosphere and Sunday morning searching for an apartment. High-rise living was the latest Vegas fad and most neighborhoods now boasted a half-completed skyscraper. There was even a two-tower condominium project aimed specifically at a gay clientele. The male tower was called Penisular and the female the Vagestic. All these high-rise compounds were completely out of her price range, though. Allie was aiming lower. Much lower.

Older apartment blocks of three or four stories prolifer-
ated on the east side of the city, near the UNLV campus.
Allie knew chipped paint, faded blinds, and broken bal-
conies meant lower rents, so it was in this area that she
began her search for somewhere affordable. The first
apartment she saw had mousetraps. The second apartment had mice. The third apartment had possibilities.

"Stallion Gate has never had any kind of random shooting," the rental agent boasted proudly. "Only domestic or
gang related. You're very lucky. This is the only unit in the
whole complex that's furnished. Mr. Garland, the former
tenant, left rather suddenly and didn't take any of his
things with him."

Allie thought she might be able to make this place
work. True, most of the furniture looked as though it
would fall apart quicker than a Hollywood marriage, but
the apartment was larger than the previous ones she had
looked at and had what the rental agent described as a
peekaboo view of the Strip. At the age of twenty-six, Allie
still had never lived alone. She had gone from her parents
to Barry to Christian. It was time she stood on her own
two Jimmy Choo's. She just had to look at her situation
with the correct perspective. This wasn't a setback; this
was a growth opportunity. Allie wrote out a check for the
first and last month's rent as well as the security deposit
and placed it in the rental agent's bony, outstretched
hand.

Allie spent the rest of her Sunday alone with a mop and
a bucket. With her long, blonde hair tied up in a scrunchie
and her manicure protected by yellow rubber gloves, she
scrubbed, vacuumed, and polished her new apartment as

thoroughly as possible. She found the work to be thera-
peutic; it was as though she was cleaning away her past
mistakes and making room for her new, single life to blos-
som through. Being dumped by Christian reminded her
of a previous emotional scar she'd endured. Matt House-
man, her first boyfriend, had quarterbacked the school
football team. Allie had been captain of the cheerleading
squad and had enjoyed basking in Matt's reflected glory.
As she tackled the green grime that had coagulated
around the kitchen taps, Allie remembered the feeling of
amputation she'd felt when Matt had moved on. Hadn't
she just repeated that experience with Christian? Well, no
more. It was time to stop subordinating herself to others.
It was time to stop cheerleading from the side and get on
the field herself. Mr. Summerford had suggested there
should be some women in upper management. Why not
her? Exhausted, she fell asleep at nine o'clock and dreamed
happily of Christian being attacked by killer mice.

A little after eight on Monday morning, Allie pulled
into her personal numbered parking space at work.
Months earlier she had arranged for her bay to be right
beside Christian's. She now cursed her nearsighted opti-
mism.

Swinging her stockinged legs out of her car and onto
concrete, she considered spitting in the space that Christian's Mercedes coupé would soon occupy. She dreaded
the embarrassing first meeting after the breakup. She had
calculated that event would most likely occur at the regular Monday-morning executive meeting due to begin in
less than an hour. Allie was determined to appear cool,
aloof, controlled, and professional. She would give Chris-

tian the warm, welcoming smile she was now practicing in the mirror of the elevator. He would never know he had parked his car on top of her imaginary spit.

Arriving at her office, Allie grabbed a cup of black coffee and an aspirin for her breakfast. Her head was throbbing relentlessly; she had a relationship hangover. During previous Monday-morning meetings, Allie had always taken her cue from Christian and backed his position on whatever issue was tabled. Their split offered her new independence. Conversely, no longer could she rely on Christian's protection; if she were to scale the corporate ladder, she was going to have to do it on talent alone.

The executive boardroom was beginning to fill up. After sneaking a cherry Danish from the sideboard, Allie sauntered casually into the room. As usual, each place at the table was set with a glass of water, a silver pencil, and a cloud-shaped notepad. Allie glanced down at her reflection in the glossy shine of the table's patina. She noticed the deep frown in the middle of her eyebrows and did her best to release it.

Christian always sat directly to the right of Richard Summerford, president and COO of Heaven. Allie always sat directly to the right of Christian. If Christian thought she would now cower at the end of the table, he was mistaken. With a flip of her hair and a swoosh of her skirt, Allie planted her size-four hips in her regular seat.

Paul Hornsucker and Orville Washington, senior vice president of casino operations and slot director, respectively, had already taken their places at the table. Slot machines were considered of such importance that they were accorded their own vice president separate from other games of chance being offered by the casino. Orville Washington was in a particularly perky mood this morning; he knew he was able to announce that the new *Desperate Housewives* slot machines would be on the floor by Memorial Day weekend, the last design tweak now in place that enabled coins to tumble out of Eva Longoria's cleavage.

Next to strut into the room was senior VP of food and beverage, Crystal Gates, carrying her usual Starbucks Venti Caffè Latte. Forty years ago, Crystal had been one of the original showgirls in the Lido de Paris show at the Stardust. Today, she was a vision in leather . . . not her clothes, her skin. Years of happily surrendering her body to the desert sun had baked her epidermis to puckered perfection. Put a handle on her head and her face could have been a handbag. Her bleached hair popped out of her scalp like fresh hay, her latex pink top accentuating her artificially enhanced, albeit slightly lopsided, bosoms.

Jimmy Falanucci suddenly appeared at the door. That was strange, Allie thought. As director of security, Jimmy never attended executive meetings.

"Morning," he said gruffly, stubbing out his fifth cigarette of the day even though it was just nine a.m.

Allie was glancing at the door, wondering if Christian was going to be a no-show, when he arrived and took his seat beside her without even a perfunctory nod of acknowledgment. Jimmy Falanucci's eyes narrowed slightly as he looked over at them. Everybody else was engaged in inconsequential chatter.

Richard Summerford's expensively suited frame filled

the doorway, followed by Senior Vice President Frank DiPaulo's slightly less-expensively suited frame tucked a touch to the right and behind. This was Frank DiPaulo's usual position. In fact, very few people had ever seen the whole Frank DiPaulo.

"Good morning," Richard said as he took his seat at the head of the table.

"Morning," said Frank, a beat quieter and later.

Summerford was overqualified for his present job. This was his eighth casino. Although it was the largest he had ever run, the challenge of running Heaven was essentially no different to the challenges he'd faced running the other seven. Richard was desperate to be bumped up to the corporate board, as it would relieve him from the detritus of detail and repetition that the day-to-day management of a casino involved. His eyes contained a constant, filmy glare of slight detachment that many misconstrued as indicative of capability, leadership, and control and that actually merely signaled boredom. He was bored with his job, bored with his marriage, bored with his life.

"First thing I'd like to discuss is our old friend revenue enhancement," he announced. "The board wants all the company's properties to amp up revenue stream in the final quarter, and as the company flagship, Heaven is expected to lead the pack."

Although Heaven's appearance to the consumer suggested profligate spending, in reality the cost control in every department was tighter than something Paris Hilton might wear on a red carpet. Showing a profit that exceeded the profit from the same period in the previous year's comparable quarter was the mantra of the new, corporate Vegas. The only way to accomplish this fiscal feat was to continually lower costs or raise revenue.

Paul Hornsucker spoke up. "My figures show gaming's up twenty percent compared to this quarter last year, Richard. Orville's done a helluva job with the new table placements. I don't see any area to further increase that stream given the number of bodies we attract."

"I agree," Richard said. "Standard casino areas are maximized. We're running at 99.8 percent occupancy. We need to think anciliary. Any ideas?"

Allie made the decision to go after Christian's tone-deaf singer. "I think the Seraphim Lounge is underachieving," she announced.

Christian whipped his head around in surprise and stared at her icily. "It's underachieving because it's under-marketed," he said archly. "We've got some great acts in there but marketing's never been able to position them properly."

"That's simply not true," Allie retorted. "The acts aren't interesting enough to attract attention from the public or the media . . . like that female singer who's in there."

Frank DiPaulo, wanting to get his voice into the minutes' report, jumped in to the discussion, saying, "Maybe we could take a look at that, Christian . . . beefing up the acts."

"Well, that would be expense enhancement rather than revenue enhancement," said a controlled but seething Christian. "For the money we pay, we have the best acts available."

"I disagree," said Allie.

If the other occupants around the table hadn't noticed a frisson between Allie and Christian before, they were certainly catching it now.

"For instance, a magic act that could not only be an evening draw but an afternoon entertainment as well might be a way to go," suggested Allie. "It would offer more entertainment hours for the same amount of money and I think it would attract more people."

"Take a look at it, Christian," ordered Richard. "But really, I'm looking for a bigger idea than just revamping the lounge. We need to come up with something that completely stuns the board."

*And gets me my bump up and more stock options,* thought Richard.

"Is there any way to make the slot machines sexier?" asked Jackson Dean, the VP of sponsorship and development.

"How do you mean?" asked Orville Washington defensively.

"Instead of sevens whirling around . . . maybe naked women? Three naked women win the jackpot . . . I know it always does for me."

An awkward silence filled the room.

"Twenty people in the room and no ideas," said Richard. "Don't make me think I've employed the wrong people."

Allie decided to speak up.

"OK, this might sound really stupid, but I've had this idea for a while and I told Christian and he said I was crazy, but I'm going to say it anyway. Weddings are one of the top-four reasons people come to Vegas, right? Why stop there?"

"Are you saying we should do divorces?" someone asked.

"No. My idea is even a little more offbeat. What else is a once-in-a-lifetime experience where people are so emotional they spend their money carelessly?"

"Bar mitzvahs?" someone guessed.

"Anniversaries?" another offered.

"Death?" joked Crystal Gates.

A chuckle began to circulate around the room, which ceased as soon as everyone saw Allie nodding her head in assent.

"OK, so maybe it was a dumb idea, but I figure a funeral's a family gathering, too. We already have the limos and the flowers. I've even got a marketing phrase: *When you die, make sure you go to Heaven.*"

There was complete silence as Allie looked around at blank faces.

"OK, I'm an idiot," she groaned.

"At least you tried," said Frank DiPaulo. "And we did say 'think outside the box' and that does involve boxes."

The chuckles of derision trailed off as Richard Summerford stood up.

"I think it's brilliant," he announced. "Well done, young lady."

Allie's smile was so wide it exposed teeth her coworkers didn't even know she possessed.

"This could open up a whole new vein of customer attraction. This could be the biggest thing since Vegas went after the convention business. A funeral's in essence a party and this is the ultimate party town," Richard enthused. He could smell the additional revenue stream and with it his promotion.

"People could leave us money in their wills to pay for the funeral," chimed in Adam Reich, the head of legal affairs, whom people referred to behind his back as Third Reich. "We could even give every guest a boilerplate addendum to their will to complete in case of their death."

"Why stop at death?" asked Richard.

"Isn't that where everything stops?" offered Crystal Gates.

"Ah, but where does it all begin?"

Allie stood up and practically yelped the answer. "Birth! YES. YES. I can see it now. *'Have your baby in Heaven. We'll deliver your little angel. Heaven's maternity wing.'* It's genius."

Allie knew calling a hotel president a genius when he's responded positively to one of your ideas was always a good move. Frank DiPaulo felt it was time to jump onto the train before it pulled out of town.

"We've created an entirely new Vegas experience. Well done, team," he crowed, including everyone in the room and therefore himself.

"What about sex after death?" asked Jackson Dean.

"Excuse me?" replied Richard.

"Well, everyone wonders what sex after death would be like, don't they?"

Jackson's eyes met the quizzical stares coming at him from every direction.

"Maybe it's even better than when you're alive. Maybe when you climax, your body just comes apart and then comes back together again. We could simulate an inner explosion."

Jackson's voice began to retreat in volume as he realized that he had gone a step too far.

"I want to put this on the fast track," Richard announced, ignoring Dean. "I want an immediate call to action. Let's pull together a research report within ten days and get a unified game plan together. Well done, Allie. Now, the other thing I wanted to discuss involves security. Jimmy, over to you."

Jimmy Falanucci stood up and walked around the table, handing everyone a ten-dollar Heaven chip. "It's not one of our chips," he said. "It's a fake."

Christian looked closely at the piece of plastic.

"It's good," continued Jimmy. "A professional forgery. So far, no other casino has reported a similar problem, so it seems that Heaven has been individually targeted. The only way to spot it is a slight weight variance, which you can only pick up if you weigh a hundred at a time."

"We haven't found many. Less than a thousand," interrupted Paul Hornsucker, "but obviously this is a big problem. We're switching out all our legitimate chips to a more sophisticated design that's considered impossible to replicate, but that won't be accomplished until the end of this month."

"So in the meantime?" asked Adam Reich. "What do we do?"

"In the meantime, we're screwed," Summerford said. "Which is why I wanted everyone to be aware of the problem. We need to get a handle on this. Maybe we'll get lucky and catch the perpetrator before we instigate the change. OK, that's it. Good meeting."

"Good meeting," echoed Frank DiPaulo, as he followed Summerford out the door.

As the group scattered to their separate workspaces, Christian summoned Allie.

"Allie, could you come to my office for a second?" Christian asked, not waiting for an answer, but walking straight toward his door.

Once Allie had come in, Christian shut the door.

"What the holy fuck do you think you're doing?" he shouted.

Allie recoiled. She had witnessed Christian's explosive temper before, but it had never been aimed in her direction.

"Wow. Guess I struck a nerve," she said. "There's no need to overreact."

Allie sounded cooler than she felt. Christian's disproportionate rage frightened her. However, she kept her game face on. "Richard has always encouraged us to reach beyond our job titles. I've told you that singer stinks and you refuse to do anything about it. Are you sleeping with her? That's the only reason I can think of that would make you keep a singer that should be fired from a shower."

Christian breathed deeply and reeled his temper back in. His extra two grand a week would disappear if Malfi disappeared from the lounge. He had to deter Allie somehow.

"She's a pretty girl, Allie. High rollers like to see pretty girls. You might get off on fifth-rate magicians you were stupid enough to marry, but Mr. Kawasaki from Japan who has just flown in on a private jet with a couple of million jingling in his pocket is not going to enjoy watching a guy pull a dove out of his ass."

"I disagree. And let's remember you're the guy who said my funeral idea stunk."

"Allie, stay out of my department's business," he warned.

"Who do you think I am? Your girlfriend?" Allie retorted. "I stopped being your ally, Christian, when you told me to move out. It's every person for him- or herself now."

"I'll try to remember that," said Christian.

"Do," said Allie, flouncing out of his office.

# SIX

"Hey, dude, wanna see a show for free?"

"No."

"How long ya gonna be in town?"

"None of your goddamn business."

"Have a great day."

"Fuck you."

Barry Houdini's first day as a pitchperson for Tropical Time-Share Resorts was not going well. Having heard nothing more from Allie about the availability of the lounge job in Heaven, Barry had decided to search for alternative employment. The time-share job had appeared simple enough when it had been described to him at the recruitment lecture.

"Three words: *Get. Them. Talking.*" The recruitment manager wrote the three magic words on a board for extra emphasis. "Fact. It's a statistical certainty that if you can get someone to talk to you, you have a fifty percent chance of getting them to hear our sales pitch. Fact. If you get them to hear our sales pitch, it's a statistical certainty we have a twenty percent chance of getting a sale. Fact. You get twenty dollars for every person you get on the bus and a thousand if your person actually buys a unit. Fact. We average a sale of four units a day. We have sixteen recruiters. So . . . Fact. One in four recruiters will make one thousand dollars a day, and all you have to do is to get someone talking. That's a fact, ladies and gentlemen. It's that easy. You can use humor. You can use charm. You can use sex appeal. You've talked to strangers before in bars, in waiting rooms, in elevators, haven't you? Now you're going to use that skill to make you and Tropical Time-Share money. Easy, huh?"

The man hitched up his pants, blinked, and paused for dramatic emphasis. Barry looked around and verified that he was still the only person at the recruitment lecture.

"What would you say if I told you we're going to make it even easier?" the man continued, reciting a speech he could now give by rote while thinking about something else entirely. As a matter of fact, at this point he was thinking about a turkey sandwich on whole wheat with extra mayo.

Listening intently, Barry couldn't understand why there weren't more people after this job. Maybe he should use the money he was going to earn to buy one of the time-shares. It seemed like a good investment.

"Tropical Time-Share has purchased at great expense a variety of tickets to wonderful, top-drawer entertainment for you to offer at absolutely zero cost as reward and incentive to people for taking our tour."

The recruiter fanned out a dozen different colored tickets to shows ranging from a lunchtime Elvis tribute to an antique car collection, all of which happened to be free, anyway.

"If they don't want a show, you can offer a top-of-the-range, luxury dining experience: all you can eat at the Senor Luau buffet. It's Mexican-Hawaiian. Delicious. You won't believe their pineapple enchiladas."

Barry nodded eagerly. He had eaten there himself. It *was* delicious.

"This is the cheese. You are the trap. Go get the mouse," the recruiter encouraged.

Brimming with enthusiasm, Barry had left the lecture and headed for the streets. So far, though, he had only managed to get two people talking. One had said, "Leave me alone"; the other had said, "Fuck you." Barry didn't think either response counted, but decided any reaction, even a rude one, was better than no reaction at all.

Tropical Time-Share Resorts had positioned Barry on a

particularly busy intersection of the Strip. This had both pluses and minuses. The obvious plus was volume. Every time the traffic lights changed, at least fifty tourists hurried across like a shoal of fish with Barry the waiting, baited hook. Barry quickly realized, though, that despite the numbers being in his favor, he could only hook one fish at a time. He also quickly realized that there was nothing more discouraging than discovering the fish you had chosen to go after either wasn't hungry or was allergic to your bait.

Barry began psychologically evaluating the people as they waited for the traffic light to turn in their favor. His new plan was to zero in on the person who looked most in need of a time-share condominium and then trap that victim as he or she reached Barry's side of the street. The problem with this theory, as Barry quickly admitted to himself as it failed for the fifth time in succession, is that people by and large fall into two mutually exclusive categories: people who have innate talent for psychologically evaluating strangers and people who stand on street corners trying to sell shit.

After three hours of laboring in the searing Nevada heat, a sticky Barry had further refined his strategy. He'd calculated that it took three minutes for the lights to change. Therefore, he spent ninety seconds walking backward with the crowd as it made its way down the Strip after crossing the lights. He issued a general invitation within the first ten seconds—"Anyone here want free tickets to a great show?"—then concentrated on anyone who showed even a glimmer of interest. If they stopped to talk, so did Barry. If he hooked nobody after ninety seconds, he ran back to the intersection so as to arrive just in time for the next group of fresh fish crossing the street. So far he had backed into the streetlight only once, although he was considering incorporating it permanently into his strategy as it had gotten a big laugh. A woman had even stopped to talk to Barry. She had asked him if he needed medical attention.

Wiping the sweat out of his eyes, Barry looked across the street at Manfred, a fellow worker, who was engaged in conversation with a woman in possession of an ass so lumpy it appeared she was using her sweatpants to transport seashells. Barry remembered that posterior from earlier this morning. Wait. There couldn't be two such rumps, could there? He recalled it being hoisted up the steps of one of the Tropical Time-Share buses that transported people to and from the tour. Barry wondered if the woman took up two seats and if that meant that Manfred got paid forty bucks. Barry was so deep in thought about the woman and her seashell ass that he let a group of fifty potential time-share customers cross the street and walk straight past him unimpeded. He could not imagine the woman actually wanting to sit through another three-hour pitch session. Barry had sat through it the day before and become so bored he'd started reminiscing about some of his old shoes. However, maybe she was so serious about buying, he reasoned, that she needed to hear about the deal again. Maybe Manfred was just a few hours away from the one thousand dollars.

Just then, Barry noticed Manfred reaching into his pocket and handing the lumpy-assed woman some money. Suddenly, it all made sense. Manfred was paying Lumpy to sit through the pitch. Pay someone five bucks, you still made fifteen. It was arithmetically perfect.

Barry changed course. Instead of looking for people who might buy a condominium, he started looking for people who might rob a condominium. On the corner was an unkempt man wearing a T-shirt that proclaimed, "I hate everyone. Even you." He was chugging a can of beer and talking to the imaginary person who lived in the can. Perfect.

"Hey, man, wanna make a couple of bucks?" Barry whispered.

"Huh?"

"I'll give you five bucks to go sit somewhere for a couple of hours," he offered.

The man looked up.

"Is there a bar?"

"No," Barry admitted.

"Forget it."

Desperate, Barry looked around for a new target. Spotting a skinny woman who was wearing what appeared to be deep-fried hair, he asked, "Excuse me ma'am, would you like to go to a buffet?"

"What kind of buffet?" the woman asked.

"Senor Luau at the Trocadero. It's Mexican-Hawaiian. Celine Dion eats there a lot," Barry improvised badly.

"OK. What time should I meet you there?"

Barry realized he had forgotten to mention that she had to go on the tour. She thought he was asking her out on a date. Barry had never been good at disappointing people.

"Seven o'clock?" he asked unhopefully.

"See you then, handsome."

The woman smiled, revealing a mouthful of confused teeth, then continued on her way.

"I've changed my mind. Make it twenty bucks and I'll go," Barry heard the drunk burp in his direction.

"Fuck you," a dispirited Barry offered back dismissively.

At that very moment, an LVPD officer pedaled by. The Las Vegas police had recently instituted a policy of using bicycles to patrol the areas of the city most highly trafficked by tourists. Unfortunately for Barry, this officer enjoyed excellent hearing.

"Is that the way Tropical Time-Shares teaches you to approach customers?" the cop asked Barry as he circled back.

"No. He's been in my face before, man. I just wanted to let him know that Vegas doesn't encourage pandering."

The drunk became offended and suddenly much more cogent. "Pandering? Officer, this guy offered me a kickback if I'd go on his shitty tour."

"I did not," Barry lied.

The Tropical Time-Share bus pulled up to the corner to board the morning's recruits. Manfred walked three people to the opened door and smiled them up the steps. This was the second Tropical Time-Share bus to leave this morning. Manfred had placed three people on each trip and Barry zero. A hollow feeling of panic gripped Barry's intestines. The bus was about to leave. Barry looked around in desperation.

"Officer, would you like a free buffet or show?"

"Tell me something, are you *trying* to get arrested?"

"No, Officer. I'm very sorry."

"Well, watch your language. I don't wanna have to tell you again."

Six hours later, a sunburned Barry handed in his resignation.

"Maybe it was just first-day jitters," said the recruiting officer. "Let me run through the facts for you again."

"I just don't think this is the job for me, man. Thanks for giving me a shot."

"Are you sure?"

"Sure. I have to go, I have a date tonight," Barry mumbled.

Unemployment, a failed marriage, and extreme poverty was a cocktail of despair that frankly would have made standing up the woman with deep-fried hair completely understandable, if not entirely excusable. After all, Barry didn't even know her name. However, Barry was not and had never been that kind of man. So he stood in front of Senor Luau's and waited. And waited. And waited, until he realized he had been stood up.

*The next morning* Barry stared hard at the HELP WANTED sign that had recently appeared in the window of his neighborhood Bouncing Bean coffee shop. He wondered if he could handle the pressure of people's coffee peccadilloes. He once heard a woman order an iced caffe latte the color of Halle Berry, with three ice cubes to be added only after the milk had been stirred clockwise vigorously for exactly one minute. Was Barry up to that sort of challenge? The smell of freshly brewed coffee mingling with the aroma of just-toasted bagels lassoed his nostrils and propelled him through the door to find out.

The first hour of Barry's trial employment went very well. He swiftly mastered both the espresso and the steam machines, and he found his magician's manual dexterity perfectly suited the rigorous demands of a delicate cappuccino. However, he feared that the more singular orders were going to be his Achilles' Venti.

"I'd like a hot soy latte, iced, please," said a woman wearing a burlap dress decorated with Indian jewelry.

"Wow, that's intense. Can you talk me through it?"

"Just make a hot soy latte and pour it over ice."

"So you want an iced soy latte?"

"No. I've told you what I want."

"Good enough. What's your name?" Barry asked, positioning his pen above a virgin cup.

"I don't give my name," the woman replied curtly.

"I'll just write 'lovely lady,'" Barry announced, determined not to have a fight.

He turned around and began mixing the concoction.

"A little more soy . . . that's enough. Are you sure that was a full shot of espresso?"

Barry tipped the hot mixture over a cup of ice and handed it to the difficult customer. "Here you go, ma'am."

The woman tasted her drink.

"It's very watery and not cold enough. Get me the manager."

"I can try again," volunteered Barry.

"No, I need to see the manager. He should know that the person making the drinks is not qualified."

Barry turned, muttering "witch" under his breath.

"Did you call me a 'bitch'?"

"No, ma'am, I called you a witch. That's different. A bitch can sometimes be in a good mood. A witch is someone who is born into a particular condition."

Moments later, Barry handed in his apron, leaving the Bouncing Bean with a stale lemon scone and a caffeine buzz in lieu of actual monetary compensation.

*Undaunted, Barry tried* a third moneymaking approach. He'd noticed that a sizable crowd always collected outside the Fashion Show mall around lunchtime.

"Do you want to see something incredible?" Barry inquired of passersby as he set fire to his sleeve. Four people formed a loose semicircle around Barry and watched as the fire disappeared and seemingly from nowhere a cooked chicken emerged. One of the pedestrians observing the performance bent down and placed a dollar on the black blanket Barry had placed on the ground.

"Thank you very much, sir," Barry called out a little too loudly to draw attention to the fact that someone had actually donated money to the Barry Fund. This sometimes guilted the remaining people watching the show to reach into their Scotch-taped wallets and throw down a wrinkled Washington.

As Barry turned around to prepare his next trick, he spotted another member of the public reaching down onto the blanket to donate a dollar.

"Thank you, ma'am."

As he turned back around and began his signature juggle—a basketball, a pool ball, and a raisin—he noticed the woman was still in a crouched position on his blanket. The woman was not depositing money; she was collecting it. "Hey, lady. You're totally missing the point here," he called out as he attempted to end the juggle. The woman quickly scampered away. His attention destroyed, Barry's juggle began to wobble, then came apart completely. Lunging, Barry caught the basketball. The pool ball, however, landed with a thunk on an audience member's head. The raisin was never found, but as far as Barry knew, did no damage.

Casting the basketball aside, Barry knelt on the blanket beside the wounded woman and said nervously, "You'll be fine. This has happened to me seven times. Look at me. I'm OK."

This time, however, Barry would not be OK. Watching the entire episode was the same policeman from the "fuck you" time-share experience.

"Street performing in Las Vegas is illegal, you know," the cop said.

"No, Officer, I didn't know."

"We're going to have to add on a charge of assault. This time, I'm going to have to take you in."

Barry shrugged defeatedly. "And I'm just gonna go with you," he replied, holding out his wrists to be cuffed.

Barry Houdini had failed Tropical Time-Shares. He had failed coffee. And he had failed juggling. He felt his life could not get any worse. He was wrong.

# SEVEN

Max Lohmann, the owner of a six-million-dollar home in Brentwood and a five-million-dollar buffalo ranch in Idaho, was at this moment sleeping on a plaid couch in his musty Burbank office. His future ex-wife, Brenda, had tossed him out and changed the locks. Years ago, Brenda had tried to "feng shui" the office, but Max had drawn a line in the dust. Now he was sleeping in it.

Max and Brenda had met at a New Jersey pizza parlor thirty-two years earlier. Brenda was a waitress. Max had owned the junk shop next door. Bosomy, big-haired Brenda was loud, fun, and crass. She was Malfi with a better voice. Their sex life had been electric. They'd made love in the backseat of Max's car so often, they had considered naming their first son Buick.

The acquisition of money is an ingredient that can dramatically alter the cocktail of life. As Max's business interests multiplied, Brenda embarked on an odyssey of self-improvement. If there was a fad or course that promised enlightenment, Brenda leaped to explore it; hers became a perpetual quest to become a different person.

Fifteen years into their marriage she convinced Max to move west: to California, land of ultimate reinvention. As if she had undergone plastic surgery of the personality, the original, fun-loving gal that Max had married had been replaced by a stern woman who rarely laughed. Brenda was a butterfly who had blossomed into a cocoon.

Max, on the other hand, was still the same guy from Jersey, albeit with a few more zeros on his bank statement. He still liked pastrami and he still liked it fatty.

"Can I have one place in this world that is the way *I* want it to be?" he had pleaded, as Brenda hung a rusty, antique God-knows-what on his office wall. "What the hell is that, anyway?"

"It's a portion of aged fence. It's from a French sheep farm," she announced.

Max eyeballed it suspiciously. "I can see it's a fence. Why are you hanging it on my wall?"

Brenda sighed, defeated. "I'll take it down."

"No, leave it up there if you like it," Max sighed back, equally defeated by the chasm that now existed between them.

His failing relationship with Brenda was not Max's only problem. His once-thriving souvenir business had turned into what he referred to as "a river of shit." Max manufactured ashtrays, key chains, cups, pens, and all those other items that display exotic destination's names on them that people buy to confirm they have actually been away from home. His company was, until recently, the leading supplier of little plastic pieces of souvenir garbage sold around the world.

The recent terrorism scares may not have dented Las Vegas' tourism but it had affected many other, less-glamorous vacation hubs. Max's earnings for the past quarter had dipped a stomach-churning 40 percent. Plus, Max was losing market share to new companies with cutting-edge ideas that made use of the latest technology. Souvenirs were no longer passive pieces of plastic. In today's world they had to have talent. They had to light up or talk or dance. The cigarette lighter could no longer just set fire to your tobacco; now it had to have a personality.

Max knew that Malfi was an expensive luxury he could no longer afford. He also knew that she was the last thing he could ever give up, even though it was getting harder and harder to scrape up the kickback that Christian Sacco demanded to keep Malfi employed at Heaven. Several weeks ago, however, flying back from an escapist weekend of enjoyment in Las Vegas, Max had pulled a ten-dollar chip from his pocket, one he had forgotten to cash in. The simplicity of the plastic laminate design caught his attention. A thought began to percolate in his mind. How hard could it be for his factory to manufacture a facsimile? Could this be a way for him to keep all the balls he was juggling safely in the air?

*A day after* seeing the counterfeit chip at the staff meeting, Christian boarded a Southwest flight from McCarran Airport to Los Angeles on the pretext that he had a meeting with agents to attend. Christian hated flying commercially, but the company jets were only made available to presidents of casinos and above. He had spotted one of Heaven's Gulfstream jets parked in a bay as his car sped past the executive airfield. It mocked him like a beautiful woman waiting for a wealthier guy to call.

Christian was rattled. For the first time, his goal of taking over Summerford's job seemed to be moving further from his grasp. He knew deep in his gut that Max Lohmann was responsible for the counterfeit chips. He'd suspected Max the moment Jimmy Falanucci had shown him the copy. Max had been betting and losing big recently, and he had just the right mix of know-how, desperation, and stupidity to attempt such a scam. If this ever got discovered by the casino, Christian knew that fat fuck Lohmann would throw him to the wolves to cut a deal. If the casino ever found out Christian was taking a kickback from Lohmann to keep Malfi in the lounge, his career would be dead. Christ, Christian might even go to prison if Richard Summerford and the board got really pissy.

Summerford was another source of worry and irritation. Who knew he'd go for Allie's dumb idea of turning Heaven into a morgue? What an asshole. But Summerford had always been susceptible to a pretty face. He'd been married to that dried-up old stick for over a million years and it affected his judgment. Maybe he wanted to bang boots with Allie.

Maybe he would. Allie was certainly capable of career sex. Christian was a testament to that. As Summerford's girlfriend, Allie would rise in the company. Who knows, she might even end up in Christian's job, or, worse still, in Summerford's. He needed to take back control.

$\mathcal{R}enting\ a\ car$ at Burbank Airport, Christian drove straight to Max Lohmann's office.

"You coulda got me fired, you stupid asshole," he barked as he stormed unannounced into Max's office. "And after all I've done for you."

"What are you talking about?" stammered Max.

"The chips, Max," Christian spat back, throwing a counterfeit chip onto the desk Max's wife had picked up in an overpriced antiques store in Belgium. "They're yours. Don't even bother to lie."

Max denied everything vehemently, but there was something about Christian's icy, impassive stare that wore him down. After five minutes of bluster, he simply ran out of bullshit.

"What can I tell you? I fucked up," Max admitted sheepishly. "My wife's got her teeth round my nutsack and my business has turned into a river of shit. I'll pay it all back. Don't make such a big deal about it."

"How many chips did you manufacture?" Christian demanded.

"Not many. And it was only tens and fifties. Nothing major. Tell me how to fix this and I'll fix it."

Christian knew the beads of sweat gathering on Max's forehead contradicted the casual tone the man was attempting to employ. "The casino knows, Max. They called me into a meeting about it."

"Look, I'll destroy the machine I made them on. And the stock of plastic. It was all a big goof, anyway. I'll pay it back and we'll forget it ever happened."

Christian said nothing. He crossed to the musty sofa, sat down, and said nothing. Max broke the silence.

"Tell me how to fix it and I'll fix it," he whispered.

"Why do you have a rusty gate on your wall?" Christian asked.

"Don't ask."

"The casino's going to make the chip design much more complicated so that it's impossible to copy."

"Well, then . . . in a way, I did them a favor."

"How's that, Max?" Christian asked sarcastically.

"I pointed out a flaw. They're fixing it. It's a win-win."

Christian smiled. "I'm not sure they'll see it like that."

"Then let's not tell them," pleaded Max.

Christian let a pall of silence fall over the room again. He brushed a speck of San Fernando Valley fluff from the knee of his suit and sighed. It was time to unveil the idea that had occurred to him somewhere over the San Bernardino Mountains.

"Max, this is your lucky fucking day. I have a suggestion that I think you'll like."

Max scooted forward in his chair. "I'm listening."

"The casino can't change the chips until the end of this month. That's eight days away."

"Uh-huh."

Christian stood up. "You only manufactured tens and fifties, huh?"

"That's right," Max confirmed.

"Can you make hundreds and five hundreds? Even one thousands? Why don't we go inside your factory and you show me this equipment?"

Now it was Max's turn to smile as he saw the direction in which Christian was heading.

"Abso-fucking-lutely. But, tell me," said Max, "if you were worried about getting busted over tens and fifties, how come you'd consider making higher denominations?"

"Let's just say I have an idea that'll divert suspicion onto someone more deserving."

"Who?" Max asked.

"Just eat the chicken, Max," Christian advised. "Don't worry about how it was killed."

# EIGHT

After being cuffed outside the Fashion Show Mall, Barry was taken downtown in a squad car and spent the night in a cell that was cleaner than his apartment. He was offered one phone call, and he made it to the only person he felt he could rely on.

In the past, Allie had imagined herself picking up her children from school, picking up groceries for her family, even picking up the dog from the groomer's. She had never, however, pictured herself picking up her ex-husband from jail.

A humiliated Barry shuffled down the steps of the downtown police station toward Allie's car. Hugging his black velvet blanket stuffed with his magic props tightly to his chest, he slid into the passenger seat beside his ex-wife.

"Thanks for getting me out of there. What a nightmare."

"What the hell did you do?"

"Nothing," Barry replied dejectedly.

"Excuse me?"

"Allie, please don't hassle me. I'm not up to it. My head feels like it's about to throw up."

"I don't think I'm hassling you. I'm picking you up from jail. As a person who cares about you, I think I deserve an explanation," Allie insisted.

Barry put his fingers to his left temple. "Is there blood shooting out of my eyes? 'Cause that's what it feels like."

Allie stopped at a red light. She and Barry watched a derelict push a shopping cart across the street.

"That could be me in a few years," Barry lamented.

"Don't be silly," Allie replied. "That's you now."

I don't think I'm getting through to you. Pretend I'm a daisy in a field. My petals are extremely loose. One gust of wind and I'm a stem . . . a dead stem."

Allie looked over at Barry. He did seem to have visibly shrunk. There was no doubt he was not in a good place—slumped in the passenger seat of a car driven by the woman who had chosen to leave him and clutching his sad, juvenile tricks to him as though they were his only source of protection.

There comes a time in every magician's life when he questions the sense of becoming a magician, when he recalls his parents' frantic attempts to explain the difference between a hobby and a profession. For Barry, that time had arrived.

"I mean, what am I even doing?" he questioned aloud. "I pull things out of one pocket and stash them in another. I palm cards. I make believe I'm sticking knives into half-dressed chicks. What kind of life is that?"

Realizing the fragility of Barry's mental state, Allie switched from scolding schoolmarm to friendly guidance counselor.

"You're an entertainer. Life can be a pretty grim proposition for a lot of people. You lift them out of their daily routine and introduce wonder into their lives."

Barry would not be mollified. "I'm a fake person with a fake job and a fake name. Barry Houdini. What a stupid thing to call myself. It's embarrassing."

Allie had been rather proud of her "wonder into their lives" phrase and was a little miffed it had received such sparse consideration. She decided it was worth repeating. "Barry Houdini brings wonder into people's lives."

"Dudes are getting shot in their homes, prostitutes are advertising on billboards, and Barry Houdini goes to jail because he's introducing wonder into people's lives. I don't think so, Allie. Introducing wonder shouldn't land you in jail."

"No, it shouldn't."

"And I don't think losing control of a pool ball should constitute assault."

"You hit someone with a pool ball?"

"Well, yeah, but she was cool with it. Everybody was cool with it," he continued, "except that cop. It was just a pool ball, it wasn't a gun."

"Perhaps you can learn something from this. Take something positive from a negative," Allie offered.

"I already have. I'm blowing this town."

Allie felt a sudden, queasy lurch attack her stomach. The involuntary physical reaction took her by surprise. "I think that would be a mistake."

"Why? There's nothing for me here. I could change my stupid name and start again. I had an idea of doing a Russian magic act. What do you think of this as a name? Warren Peace? Huh? They might eat that up in Atlantic City. Or New Zealand. I've heard that's a cool place to start over."

"I don't think that's really starting over," said Allie gently. "I think that's running away."

"Whatever."

Barry slumped down even farther in his seat. Allie wanted so badly to give him some good news she decided to make some up.

"I have something to tell you that might cheer you up."

"Nothing can cheer me up. Even you breaking up with Christian wouldn't cheer me up."

"Actually, that happened. But that isn't the good news."

"Really? You dumped him? Finally." Barry did seem cheered; color began returning to his cheeks.

"That isn't the good news," Allie repeated. "I brought up the idea of you playing the lounge at Heaven and the hotel president didn't dismiss it out of hand."

"I prefer the other news. How did he take it?"

Allie barreled ahead, embellishing a little as she went. "I'm planning to see Summerford today. I really think it's a possibility. I'm thinking more of an afternoon show to break you in and then we can possibly move into evening."

"Was he, like, completely devastated? Did he cry?"

"Barry, pay attention. I'm not talking about Christian. And not that it's any of your business, but actually it was a mutual decision."

"You mean, *he* dumped *you*?" said Barry incredulously.

Allie pulled up outside Barry's apartment. "We're here. I've got to get going. I'll call you after I talk to Summerford."

"Cool," said Barry, collecting his tricks and getting out of the car. "Who's Summerford?"

"The hotel president," said Allie impatiently. "And if I were you, rather than feeling sorry for myself, I'd go to that dump of a garage you call a workshop and start working on some new tricks."

"Will do," said a rejuvenated Barry. "Hey, Allie . . ."

But Allie had already driven away.

*Richard Summerford's office* had been decorated by his predecessor's wife. When Summerford was named the new president of the casino, a six-figure sum had been set aside as a discretionary budget item so that Richard could personalize his new territory. However, he had opted to add the money back into his first fiscal quarter in charge. As he anticipated, the board had been suitably impressed by their new man's frugality.

Richard's motive was not entirely intended to curry

favor within the company, although that was a welcome bonus. It was simply based on his suspicion that the former president's wife had better taste than his own. Richard's last office, which *had* been decorated by his wife, had ended up looking like an igloo. Cindy, the high-school sweetheart Richard had married twenty-five years ago, had ordered everything painted a stark white. A molded rounded ceiling and bear rugs on the floor had completed the frozen effect.

"I love it," Richard had deadpanned the first time he had entered the room. "All I need is a fishing rod, a hooded parka, and a dead whale, and I'll be one happy Eskimo."

Cindy was not amused, and it took a pair of particularly lovely and expensive Fred Leighton earrings before Richard was welcomed back into the matrimonial bed. Anxious not to upset his wife again and risk having to buy the matching necklace, Richard had shivered in that office for three years. This workspace, with its mahogany-paneled walls, dark leather interior, and multiple flat-screen TVs, was much more to his liking. Richard had merely added the few awards he had received for excellence in his field, his squash trophies from college, and photos of Cindy and their almost-handsome twin sons, and pronounced himself happy.

Now, reclining backward in his high-backed, teak-bordered, leather executive chair, Summerford stared at the four television screens that stared back at him throughout his day. The news, the stock tickers, the weather, and the Home Shopping Network were his constant office companions. The news informed him; the stock tickers enriched him; the weather comforted him; and the Home Shopping Network relaxed him. He jotted down the order number of the robotic vacuum cleaner that promised to clean behind the sofa and underneath the bookcase. There were already four thousand sold and only two minutes left to place an order that included free shipping. Richard wondered if he had time to phone before his appointment with Allie Bowen. He picked up the phone and entered his personal shopping number. His order was confirmed only moments before Allie knocked on the door.

"Thank you so much for seeing me, Richard," she said breathlessly, stepping forward and occupying the seat in front of his desk.

"Can I get you something, Allie? Water? Coffee?"

"Water would be great."

Richard walked over to the concealed bar hidden behind one of the wall panels and selected a bottle of refrigerated Heaven water and a glass. Richard liked Allie. He thought she had potential. He liked the way she'd handled that unfortunate incident in the lobby with the jumper earlier that month. She was smart. And she was hot. Richard had noticed recently how much he found almost all women young enough to be his daughter terribly attractive. Of course, he knew Allie had been seeing Christian. Richard felt she could do better. Allie was going to go far. Diversity was the latest upper-management buzzword, and maybe it was time for a female president. With his support, maybe Allie could be that person in a few years' time.

"Here," said Richard, placing the glass and a napkin in front of his visitor. "Now, what can I do for you?"

Allie leaned forward and lowered her voice. "You always told us not to give up on our ideas if we really believed in them."

Summerford leaned forward and lowered his voice as well.

"Yes . . . I was only kidding." Richard smiled; ordering the vacuum robot had put him in a playful mood.

Allie laughed, hoping that he was kidding about kidding. "I know you think revamping the lounge is a small idea, but I believe it's the smaller ideas that make a casino a place people want to revisit. It's the tiny connections you make to a property that foster a commitment. You've always stressed, Richard, that return business and customer loyalty is the linchpin of a casino's operating plan."

"It is."

"I know you're looking for big ideas like my funeral concept . . ."

"Revolutionary," Summerford interrupted. "I think it's going to be huge."

"Thank you," continued Allie. "But in entertainment, sometimes the best big ideas emerge from a successful little idea that blossoms into something big. Siegfried and Roy started as a speciality act in Lido de Paris. Magic has always worked in this town because it's not language specific."

Summerford leaned forward. Allie assumed she was doing well and so chose that moment to pull some papers out of her folder. In actual fact, Richard was just getting a better angle so he could see how the stock market was doing.

"Christian hates this guy because he's my ex-husband,"

she said matter-of-factly. "I think that's shortsighted. And I'm not pitching him because he's my ex-husband. I'm pitching him because he has great potential."

"In actual fact," said Summerford as he began flicking through the portfolio of Barry's press clippings that Allie had collated, "being your ex would suggest he was the last person you'd want to help."

"Exactly," exclaimed Allie, happy to accept any advantage. "In plain terms, Christian's singer is a disaster. Here's a graph of the bar receipts during her act as opposed to the act who goes on before her. My guy can work afternoons *and* evenings *and* he'll do better. And he'll work for less."

"Does he have a lot of props? The key to a lounge act is being eye-catching enough to pull people into the bar."

"He has a workshop full of material. He builds all his stuff himself. He's very creative." Allie mentally crossed her fingers. Barry may not have many completed props now, but he would once she got through with him.

"Have you talked to Christian about this?"

"Christian and I broke up. That's why I had to come and see you. I feel that Christian's personal animosity toward me is stopping him from doing the right thing for the casino."

Richard glanced up; the NASDAQ was up ten points. Excellent. "Personally, I've always liked magic. It not only crosses languages, it crosses generations. The only demographic you miss is the blind, and there aren't that many of them in Vegas. I'll talk to Christian and get us all on the same page. I'll make it happen."

Allie couldn't believe her luck. "Thank you, Mr. Summerford," she gushed. "I really appreciate you giving me this time."

"You're very welcome," said Richard, rising from his chair to indicate the meeting was over. "By the way, have you ever tried one of those robotic vacuum cleaners?"

Allie blinked. Robotic vacuum cleaners? What was he talking about?

"Umm, no. Not really."

"OK, just wondered."

"Are you thinking of them for the guest's rooms?" she asked.

"No, but that's not a bad idea, either, young lady. I have high hopes for you."

"Thank you," said a confused Allie as she left.

Alone again, Richard glanced at his watch and then back up at his beloved televisions. He had ten more minutes before his next meeting. The market was up, the news was old, the weather was good, and the shopping network had segued into a presentation of seven transparent pots that took the guesswork out of cooking. Richard wasn't interested in them. He already had a set. They were good.

# NINE

On his flight back from Los Angeles, doubts and qualms about his plan began to fester in Christian's mind. Could he go through with it? Could he accept the inevitably unpleasant repercussions? Christian was not a man who believed in an afterlife or eternal accountability. So he rationalized that any feelings of guilt he possessed were entirely irrational, created by a rule book he neither believed in nor acknowledged. Why then was he hesitant?

"I stopped by the Seraphim Lounge to see that girl who's in there now," Summerford told Christian as soon as he returned to his office. "I gotta tell you the truth, Christian . . . I'd rather listen to a car alarm."

"She's an acquired taste."

"So's my wife's cooking, but it's still lousy. Allie thinks this magician might work. Apparently he's got a work-shop full of tricks."

Allie had once told Christian about the garage be-hind Industrial Road that Barry referred to as his work-shop and which contained half-thought-out tricks and quarter-finished props. They had lain in bed and laughed about Barry's plan to saw a real monkey in half.

"It just might be the sort of thing the lounge needs to stop underperforming."

"But, I really think—"

"This isn't worth us disagreeing over, Christian," Christian's boss interjected with a tone of finality. "Just action it, please. I realize you've had personal problems with Allie, but I think she's got star potential."

"She's very talented," Christian said tersely.

"Very," agreed Richard. "I know the company is big on diversity. We need more female executive officers here at Heaven. Let's give Allie a shot."

Christian felt his sphincter tighten.

"You'd better watch your step," Summerford joked. "You never know, you may end up working for your ex-girlfriend."

Christian attempted a smile.

Seeing Christian distressed, Summerford decided to throw him a bone. "By the way, Christian, I have to go to Bangkok next month to check out a potential new restaurant. Wanna come?" he asked.

Christian fully realized that this trip was being offered as a consolation prize. He also realized that sixteen hours alone with Richard on a company jet would be a perfect opportunity to advance his candidacy as Richard's successor. "I'd love to," he said.

"Great. I hear they have some way-out clubs there, too," Richard mentioned as he stood. "Maybe we'll find some entertainment ideas as well."

"Maybe."

With that, the men shook hands and parted. Christian was now completely determined to implement his scheme. Given his conversation with Summerford, no other course made sense.

*The evening that* followed was one of those meteorologically irresponsible Vegas summer nights when it feels as though the sun has forgotten to go down and is really just hiding behind the moon. Christian consulted his Mercedes' dashboard and noted that, despite the fall of darkness, the air temperature outside was still well over a hundred degrees.

He turned the car's air-conditioning to tornado as he drove through the airport-tunnel bypass and aimed all the blowers directly onto his face. Driving toward his arranged rendezvous with Jimmy Falanucci, he phoned Allie on his cell. Allie surprised him by still being at work at nine o'clock.

"Allie Bowen."

"It's me. You're still there? I was going to leave you a message."

"Yes?"

Even with a bad connection, Christian could detect the refrigerant in Allie's voice.

"I'm calling to apologize. I'm sorry. I overreacted about your comments at the meeting last week."

"I guess Summerford must have spoken to you," said Allie coldly.

Christian sensed his clumsy attempt at conciliation was not working, just as he had hoped.

"This is a lousy connection; I really am sorry. Have lunch with me tomorrow," he cajoled. "We can talk about possibly putting Barry in the lounge."

" 'Possibly'?"

Christian held his temper.

"Don't bust my balls, Allie. I'm going to do it. I just have to iron out some details. One o'clock at Pandora's sound good?" Pandora's Lunchbox was the coffee shop in Heaven. Christian and Allie had enjoyed eating there together in happier times.

"One fifteen," Allie countered.

Christian took a deep breath and concentrated on the bigger picture. "One fifteen," he confirmed.

Christian's coupé glided expensively down the 215 toward Henderson. Henderson was the older of Las Vegas' two key residential suburbs. Falanucci lived somewhere near the Sunset Station Casino on Sunset Road.

Christian had arranged to meet him in one of his favorite new establishments. A Little Off the Top was an open-all-night topless hair salon. It was a brilliant concept; Christian was annoyed he hadn't thought of it himself.

At Christian's suggestion, Jimmy was getting a pedicure from a jiggling pair of 32Ds.

"Relax," said the pedicurist. "This is supposed to make you less nervous, not more."

"I'm not nervous," Jimmy assured her.

In fact, Jimmy *was* nervous, but not because of the bare breasts swaying in front of him or the hands kneading his feet. He was nervous of what was going to be asked of him by Christian Sacco. Jimmy knew he was Christian's "Get Out of Jail Free" card, and he knew Christian had finally come to collect. It killed Jimmy that he owed such a colossal debt to a pig like Christian, but he did, and there was nothing he could do about it. He had not been surprised when he had received the call earlier that day summoning him to a clandestine meeting. The only surprise to Jimmy was that the payback had taken so long.

"How are you, buddy?" Jimmy heard, feeling a conspiratorial squeeze on his left shoulder. "Thanks for meeting me like this."

Christian casually sat next to Jimmy and removed his shoes and socks. Jimmy had once envied Christian his good looks. Now, however, Jimmy noticed that despite the immense personal care and expensive wardrobe Christian had always lavished on his appearance, time and character had added a pinched sharpness to the casino executive's features that today lent him an unappetizing, rodentlike quality.

"How good is this?" Christian groaned with happiness as his feet were slipped into warm, soapy water by a well-endowed, half-naked girl named Brooke. "Isn't it the best?"

Jimmy turned to face Christian directly. "What can I do for you, Christian?" he asked, wanting to establish that this was a business meeting and not a social one.

Christian got the message. "I need a favor."

"I want to do you one."

"Excellent. Give us a moment, Brooke."

As Brooke scampered away, Christian said in a low voice, "I need some machinery being freighted in from LA to be picked up at the airport and taken to a garage. Quickly and quietly."

"That it?"

"It's a surprise delivery; the garage is going to be locked. I need someone who can get in and out without leaving any footprints. Know anyone who can do that?"

"Sure. Me."

"Thanks, Jimmy."

"If I do this for you, this makes us even, right?"

"We'll see, Jimmy. We'll see."

There it was. Even after doing this favor, Jimmy would still remain under Christian's thumb because of what had happened in Atlantic City over a decade ago. Jimmy realized that the only way he was ever going to wriggle out of Christian Sacco's control was by getting as much dirt on the man as the man had on him. Tipping his pedicurist, Jimmy left the salon and climbed into his truck. With exaggerated care, he set his ball cap down on the passenger seat, anxious not to disturb the concealed device it contained.

# TEN

Pandora's Lunchbox was one of Heaven's more casual eateries. Christian dined there often, as he found both the speed of service and the sesame noodles appealing. Allie arrived there at exactly 1:15, determined to play the cool professional.

"If this is ever going to work," began Christian, "we have to separate our professional lives from our private lives. I'll admit I made a mistake about Barry. He's a really good idea for the lounge. I let my personal feelings cloud my judgment."

"So you do have personal feelings," Allie sniped. "I wasn't sure you were capable of them after the way you've been behaving."

Christian realized he would have to do more than imply some form of verbal concession if this conversation was to go in the direction he needed it to go. "I miss you, Allie," he lied. "Separating from you is the hardest thing I've ever done. If I've been prickly lately, it's because this breakup's been tougher on me than I thought it would be."

Allie knew this was as close as Christian could ever come to admitting he'd made a mistake. She felt a little better knowing he had suffered.

"Let's talk about Barry," said Allie, sitting up straight and staring directly at him. "Three grand a week, one-year guarantee, and the standard entertainer perk package. And don't try to haggle. Remember, I know how much you've been paying Malfi Molini."

"How many shows?" asked Christian.

"Two a day, Sundays dark."

"Two a day every day and four weeks off a year," countered Christian. "I'll offer those four weeks to Malfi as part of her kiss-off."

Allie was surprised at the ease of the negotiation, but

figured that Barry was the beneficiary of the guilt Christian was feeling about the way he had treated her.

"Done. Let's order lunch."

Two cosmopolitans later, Allie was giddy at their just-like-old-times conviviality. If only Christian would always behave like this, Allie was sure they could have had a future. It was a little after two when Christian remembered the Tuesday senior-staff management meeting.

"Shit," he said, looking at his watch and jumping up from the table. "I'm late. And I was supposed to change some chips for Richard. Now I'm really going to be late."

"Can I help?" Allie offered, hoping to demonstrate her broad-minded detachment.

"Would you? I need these cashed for some high-roller friend of Richard's that's on a six p.m. flight back to the Bahamas."

Christian pulled a manila envelope full of one-thousand-dollar chips out of his jacket pocket and handed it over to Allie.

"There's twenty grand there. Cash them out at the cage."

"Shall I bring it to your meeting?" Allie asked.

Christian thought about it.

"No," he said, finally. "Leave it in your office and I'll pick it up from you later. I'm glad we did this. It was nice." Christian leaned down and kissed her on the cheek. "Sign the bill to my comp number. God, I'm late."

Allie watched as his broad shoulders disappeared into the lobby. Maybe Christian was still capable of becoming the man she believed he could be. Even though he was ten years older than she was, he needed time to mature. If she was still available once he'd made that emotional journey, who knew what might happen?

Two hours later, Christian phoned from his car.

"It's me," he said to Allie. "I had to go off property for a thing. Did you cash those chips?"

"Of course, Christian," Allie confirmed. "Happy to help out."

"I really appreciate it. The guy left on an earlier flight, though. Can you just hold on to the money until I get back?"

"Not a problem."

"Great. Thanks. You're terrific. I mean that. By the way, Richard signed off on Barry. I'll e-mail you a deal memo in the next twenty-four."

"Thanks. Barry will be thrilled."

"Nothing I like better than making the day of my exlover's ex-husband," Christian replied jokingly.

Christian clicked off the phone. He had one more job for Falanucci and then his plan would be complete. He began to dial Jimmy's number.

*Eight hours later,* Allie was called back to the casino. At first she thought it was a practical joke when security officers surrounded her car as she pulled into her parking space. Then, being brusquely and wordlessly led through the basement corridors of the casino, she reconsidered. It wasn't a joke. It was a mistake. She was confident Richard Summerford would sort it all out as soon as he was called to the interview room she had been placed in. And once he'd discovered who had inconvenienced his new protégé, someone would get fired.

But it hadn't happened like that. It had unfolded like a living nightmare and Allie was still experiencing it. She stared in disbelief at the roll of one-hundred-dollar bills that had been found in her handbag. It lay beside the pile of counterfeit chips Richard Summerford had poured accusingly onto the table in front of her. How could those have been found in her office? It made no sense.

"I want a lawyer," Allie repeated forcibly.

She glanced at Christian. Summerford, in the chair opposite, stared icily at her. "OK, Allie," he stated formally. "We can get you a lawyer. Then I'll call the police. Or, we can handle this internally."

"Richard, I'm being framed," a trembling Allie insisted, jerking her chin in Christian's direction. "He gave me those chips at lunch and told me to change them for a friend of yours. They were in a manila envelope. That envelope there."

Allie pointed to the envelope lying on the table that she had stuffed into her handbag after visiting the casino cage.

"Allie, don't. Everyone here knows the truth," pleaded Christian. "Listen to Richard. If he goes to the police, you'll go to prison. Please just calm down. You know I'll do whatever I can to help."

Summerford stood up and marched wordlessly toward the casino's security center. As he swung the door open, one of the security officers who had been busy taping movies from the hotel's in-room pay-per-view quickly attempted to conceal his activity. Striding intently toward

Jimmy Falanucci's office, Summerford didn't even notice him.

"When and where did you have lunch?" Summerford asked Christian, brusquely.

"Pandora's Lunchbox. I got there about one fifteen and left an hour or so later."

"Jimmy, do you have a tape of Pandora's Lunchbox?"

"Sure, Boss."

Jimmy's heart sank. He had wondered why Christian had called last night and asked for this particular tape. As Summerford and Falanucci watched the video, Christian stood quietly in the shadows of the back of the room.

"She's lying," Summerford announced at the conclusion of the tape, which now showed only an amicable lunch between the two former lovers.

"She has to have had a partner, Richard," Christian whispered. "Give me ten minutes alone with her and I'll get the truth. Just her and me. Don't call the police. She fucked up, but she's not a bad person. Cut her some slack. For me."

Jimmy Falanucci felt like puking, but stayed dumb.

"She leaves today," spat Summerford. "She never works in a casino again. I want all the details of the scheme and a letter of resignation on my desk within the hour. Otherwise we prosecute."

"Sure, Boss."

Christian sauntered back to the holding room. He entered and dismissed the guard.

"I've thought of a flaw in your plan," Allie snarled triumphantly. "There are cameras in Pandora's Lunchbox. We're on tape."

"Richard and I just watched the tape, Allie," said Christian dispassionately. "There's nothing on it that incriminates me."

Allie's shoulders slumped. "You unbelievable prick! How did you do that?"

Christian was beside her now, and leaned in close. "Did you honestly think I'd let you treat me like that?" he spat into her left ear. "Going over my head? Making me look stupid in a meeting? Trying to get the job that's rightfully mine?"

Allie stared at Christian, incredulous. He was framing her because she spoke out in a meeting?

"Do you know anything about me at all, you dumb bitch?"

"I know you're an asshole."

Christian stepped back. Aware of the security cameras in the room, which he correctly guessed Summerford had ordered to be switched back on, he said, in his most conciliatory tone, "Richard has asked that you sign a letter of resignation. He has also asked me to tell you that you are never to work in another casino in Nevada again. If you do, he will report you to the Gaming Commission and he'll be forced to prosecute."

Allie considered her options. They didn't exist.

"What about Barry? The job?"

"You worry about you, Allie. Don't worry about Barry."

Defeated, Allie voiced no objection.

An hour later, Christian delivered the signed letter in person to Richard Summerford.

"She won't give up her accomplice, but I think I know who it is," Christian told Summerford.

"Who?"

"Her ex-husband. I bet that's why she was trying to get him a job here. With two of them on the property it would make their scam easier to operate."

"Him I will send to prison," said Richard Summerford matter-of-factly.


*Allie sat slumped* in her rented apartment and sobbed. A cardboard box containing her meager office belongings lay on the cheap, chipped coffee table in front of her. She was furious with Christian, furious with Richard Summerford, furious with the casino, but mostly, she was furious with herself for not anticipating Christian's duplicity. She had tried to phone Barry three times to tell him the job offer no longer existed, but had got his machine each time. She was about to try his number again when her cell phone rang. She opened it up and heard Barry's voice.

"Barry, I screwed it up. The job at Heaven isn't going to happen. I'm so sorry."

"I've got bigger problems, Allie. I'm back in jail."

"What? How could you perform again without a permit? I don't believe you," said an exasperated Allie.

"No." Barry's voice sounded hollow and frightened. "It's worse than that."

Barry told his ex-wife about his Kafkaesque morning: how the police had broken into his apartment and taken him downtown; how they had told him about the counterfeiting equipment they had discovered in his garage workshop; how they had told him he was definitely going to prison. Allie listened, horrified.

"It's Christian," she croaked. "He did this." Grabbing her car keys, she rushed out of the apartment and headed for Heaven.

Thirty minutes later Jimmy Falanucci was informed by one of his staff that Allie Bowen had entered the property, leaving her car parked untidily on the sidewalk under the hotel's porte cochere. He put a call into Richard Summerford.

"I want her eighty-sixed from the property," Summerford ordered.

Jimmy reluctantly dispatched two security officers to put the hotel president's order into motion. The officers and Allie arrived at Christian's office within thirty seconds of each other.

"You fucking evil bastard!" Allie screamed at Christian. "How could you do that to Barry?"

Christian remained impassive behind his desk even as Allie raised her fists to strike him. He grabbed both her arms as they descended and twisted her body to the floor.

"Don't be so stupid, Allie," he commanded. "This is the problem with women. They always get overemotional and irrational when you no longer want to fuck them."

Allie bit into the fleshiest part of Christian's thigh.

"Ow! You fucking bitch!"

He threw her hard onto the floor and the two security guards corralled her. Allie attempted to spit at Christian, but only succeeded in dribbling down the front of her Jaeger suit.

Christian inspected his leg, more dismayed to find Allie's teeth had torn his Yves Saint Laurent pants than at the pain of the bite.

"You crazy, crazy bitch! Will you look at what you did?"

"Next time I'll bite higher," Allie threatened as the security guards began dragging her out of the room.

"Bye, Allie," said Christian superciliously, as her high heels dragged backward across the carpet. "Be sure not to write."

Christian walked to his office door and closed it shut. Rubbing his leg, he limped over to his humidor, selected one of his special Monte Cristo cigars, cut it, and lit it. He felt content and relieved. It was over. Christian had increased both his and Max Lohmann's bank accounts substantially while at the same time keeping Malfi in the lounge to supply weekly cash flow to support his increasingly expensive lifestyle. All it had cost was one ambitious ex-girlfriend and a shitty magician. It was the kind of trick Barry Houdini could only dream about.

# ELEVEN

Unable to make bail, Barry languished in the Clark County Detention Center, booked on seven counts of fraud. His court-appointed lawyer was anxious to avoid a judge and jury. "We *could* go to trial, Barry," he hedged. "But there's a wealth of circumstantial evidence against you."

"I didn't do anything," Barry protested yet again.

"I'm confident I can plea-bargain this down to an eighteen-month sentence," the lawyer advised. "You could be out in less than a year."

Imprisonment for less than a minute for a crime he knew he hadn't committed seemed way harsh to Barry. "If we go to trial, you might have an eighty percent chance of acquittal," Barry's lawyer continued.

"Sounds good to me," Barry interrupted.

"That means a twenty percent chance of a guilty verdict and a ten-to-fifteen-year sentence. Juries make mistakes. People don't want to believe that, but it's true. Look at O.J. Trust me. Take the deal, Barry," the exasperated lawyer insisted.

Later that day, Barry told Allie, "I'm going to accept the plea bargain."

"What? But I can tell them what happened. I can tell them the truth," Allie told her ex-husband, looking at him through glass that needed cleaning and speaking to him through a phone that needed disinfecting.

"My lawyer thinks that's a bad idea. He says you're not credible."

"But I have to have my day in court. I'm entitled to it."

"This isn't about you, babe," said Barry softly.

Allie felt like crying but couldn't; she was all cried out. She had lost twelve pounds since the day she had been kicked out of Heaven and she was sure eleven of those pounds had been lost through tears. "You're right," she whispered. "I'll do whatever you say. And I'll visit you whenever I can."

"No visits," said Barry firmly. "I don't want you to see me in there, Allie. I don't want you to see me like that."

"I'll write every day, then," she promised vehemently. "And I'll make as much money as possible while you're in there so you can get a fresh start once you're released."

"That'd be cool. You take care of you," Barry said softly. "I'll be OK."

"Can't you just shout at me?" Allie begged. "This is completely my fault and you're being so incredibly reasonable about it all."

"Look," said Barry. "It's not like my life wasn't messed up already. Maybe this will spit me out into a better place."

"But I've seen prison in the movies," said Allie. "I'm so worried about you."

"I'm tougher than you think," smiled Barry, knowing the opposite to be true. With a sad smile he put his head to the glass partition in a gesture of farewell. Time was up.

Allie had wallowed in self-pity for over a month now, waiting for the phone call that would right the injustice that had been done to her: *Sorry, Allie. Turns out you did nothing wrong. Would you like your old job back? By the way, we executed Christian this morning.*

That phone call had never come. Allie's plan to tell her version of what happened at Barry's trial had been thwarted as well. There would be no trial. Barry's lawyer was right; justice was untrustworthy, unreliable, and fickle.

Outside the Clark County Detention Center, Allie vomited volubly into a nearby trash can. What had caused everything to go so terribly wrong? She had been so sure the move from her childhood home in Iowa to exciting Las Vegas was the right thing to do, despite her parents' misgivings. She had been determined to marry Barry even though her parents had expressly forbidden it. She had been equally sure that leaving Barry for Christian was the right move. Now, at twenty-six, the deficit of her bad choices writ large, she was unsure of everything except that her life was a complete mess.

*Allie retreated to* her crappy apartment, locked the door, turned on the TV, and let the hair on her legs grow. Days passed in a haze of sameness. One afternoon a particularly poignant episode of *Dr. Phil*, featuring a quadriplegic who had graduated from law school so she could help other victims of drunk drivers, pulled Allie out of her funk.

She resolved to pickle no longer in victim juice. A bad thing had happened to her. So be it. Worse things had befallen less-deserving people. She had an obligation to help Barry and a burning, furious desire to get even with Christian. Those were the two searchlights by which she would now navigate her life.

Allie downsized yet again, moving to an even less-expensive apartment. Eating well on a budget in Las Vegas was entirely possible, given the number of reasonably priced buffets in town. For four dollars and ninety-nine cents Allie could not only get "all she could eat," but all she could surreptitiously stuff into her handbag as well. She was pretty sure that her savings would get her through the next few difficult months, but they wouldn't get Barry a new start. What Allie needed was serious cash. What she needed was a plan.

Ninety percent of the jobs advertised in the employment section of the paper were casino related. Christian had seen to it that Allie could not get employed in any Las Vegas casino, not even the ones in the outer suburbs that catered to locals and truck drivers. The other even semidesirable jobs required schooling that Allie either didn't have or didn't have the time to acquire. She had a deadline. She needed a job that would pay her so well that when Barry was eventually released, she would be able to give him the starting-over nest egg he deserved.

Scouring the classifieds in the *Las Vegas Review-Journal* one morning, sitting in her local Laundromat in front of her rapidly rotating clothes, Allie heard a voice ask, "Allie? Allie Bowen?"

She looked up to see Angela Porter, the woman whose job Allie had taken at Heaven almost two years earlier.

"Angela!" Allie should have felt guilty. She had, after all, started as Angela's assistant and had put up zero resistance when management had decided to ax Angela and upgrade Allie. However, Angela was looking so unbelievably great that it was difficult for Allie to muster up any emotion other than envy. Angela had always been extremely attractive, which made her perfect for public relations work. With her dazzling smile, long, brunette hair that ended just above her heart-shaped butt, pert 34C boobs, and legs that went on forever, she was sometimes mistaken for Catherine Zeta-Jones. Two years later, she still looked like a knockout. She was expensively dressed and evenly tanned and looked somehow different. Allie couldn't quite put her finger on the source of the difference, and then she realized what it was: Angela looked wealthy.

"Can you believe my washing machine at home broke down?" said an exasperated Angela. "Eight thousand dollars a month this condo is costing me and the washing machine packs up. Oh, they can get to it by next Tuesday, but what am I supposed to do until then? Wear dirty clothes and scratch?"

"Eight thousand dollars?! Where on earth are you living?" asked Allie.

"Tournament Place," said Angela.

Tournament Place was quite possibly the ritziest address in Las Vegas. Right on the Strip, it was an enclave of high-rise luxury apartments surrounding a private club. Allie had attended a party there once with Christian and had been duly impressed by the clubhouse, whose gold ceiling had been flown in from France and whose marble floor had traveled from Italy. On top of that, the lobster had been flown in from San Francisco and the caviar from Russia. Allie remembered thinking that just by standing there and eating the food she should be entitled to frequent-flier miles.

Angela opened the dryer next to Allie's and started to pile her wash into it. Allie noticed that Angela's laundry seemed to consist mainly of the briefest of sparkly thongs and matching bras. "Wanna go next door and grab a coffee?" asked Angela, pressing the delicate, slow-spin cycle as she inserted coins into the machine.

"Sure," said Allie, interested to find out what it was that

Angela was doing that allowed her to live at Tournament Place. Allie was unprepared for Angela's response.

"I'm a dancer at Leopards," Angela announced over a cappuccino.

Leopards was one of the largest strip clubs in town. Allie unsuccessfully tried not to look shocked.

"Please. This is Vegas. You think it's gambling that makes this city different? They have gambling in Des Moines. It's sex that makes Vegas Vegas, Allie, and if you've got the necessary physical attributes, it's nuts to live here and not exploit them."

Allie couldn't help but offer up an argument. "But dancing in front of those sleazy men? Doesn't it make you feel—?"

"Empowered," interrupted Angela. "That's how it makes me feel. First time I did it, it was a total thrill."

"Really?" said Allie, intrigued. "You don't feel cheap?"

"No, honey, I don't feel cheap. I feel expensive. The best thing that ever happened to me was you taking my job in Heaven. I'd even thought about writing you a thank-you note."

Allie laughed and sat up a little straighter. She was unsure how far she could pry, but she definitely wanted to know more.

Angela, however, needed little prompting. "The nine-to-five grind, knowing you might get a hundred-dollar raise in two years and the pressure of working for other people, was just killing me. At Leopards, I'm responsible for how much money I make. And I make a lot."

"You don't have to pay the club?"

"Fifty bucks a night house fee, and after that, I keep

everything. There are over four hundred girls working in the club on any given day, and nobody's walking out with less than five hundred bucks a night, cash. I'm going to make almost half a mil this year."

Allie was shocked and almost choked on her cappuccino.

"What's happening in Heaven these days?" Angela asked.

Quickly editing the past month's events in her mind, Allie came up with a new version. "I got tired of it, too. I left a month ago. It's a glass ceiling for women, isn't it?"

"Yeah, it's not like that in Leopards," Angela replied. "There it's a glass floor."

Allie laughed uneasily, not knowing whether or not she was joking.

"I'm not kidding. You have to be very comfortable with your body to work there. But there's nothing as nice as a load of cash and total independence. Are you interested?"

Allie *was* interested, but dancing naked was not something she needed to add to her list of bad life choices.

"I don't think I could do it," said Allie. "Correction—I know I couldn't do it."

"Well, if you ever change your mind, I'm there most nights. Feel free to come check it out."


Barry Houdini had thought he'd known fear before in his life. He remembered a gang of older boys surrounding him on the playground and bullying him until he gave up his baseball. And he remembered falling out of a tree at the age of ten and hearing the snap of his ankle breaking beneath him. But Barry realized that the sort of fear he was feeling now, as he sat shackled in an airless prison transport bus, was an entirely new plateau of terror. He attempted to remain rigid. He instinctively suspected that showing any sign of weakness to his seven cotravelers would cost him dearly later.

Barry was already aware how much he stood out. For one thing, he had no tattoos. The majority of people on the bus were covered in tattoos. Barry snuck a look at the convict opposite him. Permanent ink covered his skin from his neck down to both wrists. The man's bare arms were covered in snakes, skulls, and swastikas, and prominently displayed on his left bicep were the initials SWP: Supreme White Power. Barry wondered what the smiling black guy sitting directly behind thought of that.

"Who you eyeballin', punk-ass bitch?" spat the Nazi skinhead suddenly, whipping his shaved head around at Barry.

"Wh . . . what?" stammered Barry.

"You stop looking at me, you skinny-fish motherfucker, else I'll peel your fuckin' onion."

Even though he had no idea what that meant, Barry felt a small trickle of urine descend his left leg as the Nazi continued to stare malevolently. Barry knew he was a goner. Just then, the black guy immediately behind the Nazi spoke up.

"Yo, who do we have to fuck to get some AC, dawg? It's hotter than a crack ho's mouth in here."

Everybody laughed, including the tattooed Nazi and the prison guard escort who sat up front in the van with the driver, secure behind the Plexiglas partition replete with heavy-gauge metal mesh.

"Whatchu down for this time, dawg?" the prison guard asked the joker.

"Got a fucking nickel for a PV that was pure bullshit, know what I'm sayin'?"

"Yeah, yeah. Whatever, dawg," the prison guard responded world-wearily.

"It's a muthafuckin' conspiracy against the black man, that's what it is."

More laughter. Barry was completely lost, and surprised that the patois of the guard and the guarded seemed so similar, but he was grateful that the exchange had distracted the Nazi.

With the conversational ice broken, more chatter bubbled up in the van, and Barry felt at ease enough to turn around and look at his other fellow prisoners. Each possessed a sad, sallow complexion and greasy-haired uniformity that suggested the entire group had originated from the same inbreeding trailer park located somewhere in Nowheresville, USA.

"There it is," groaned one of the white boys, pointing his straggly goatee toward the van's windscreen.

Barry looked ahead and saw the lonely, nightmarish vista silhouetted against the horizon. A razor-wired prison compound enclosed with concentric circles of fences, punctuated on each corner with a forbidding gun tower, loomed ahead.

"It's all good," said the black guy cheerily to nobody in particular. "It's all good in the hood."

Ten minutes farther slog through the brown, desolate landscape, the van came to a stop at the checkpoint guardhouse. The driver lowered his window and barked, "Incoming! Eight fish, Clark County!"

The gates swung open. The van pulled into a small yard of dirt and sand before coming to a halt beside a grimy, two-story cellblock that looked as though it had been fashioned out of moldy Swiss cheese.

A clipboard-carrying guard in a khaki uniform entered the van. "LISTEN UP, YOU FUCKIN' JERK-OFFS! I am the intake sergeant. I am here to get you sorry bunch of dickheads situated in the Fish Tank. Gen pop is currently full, so you're gonna be here at least a month."

The other inhabitants of the van started griping.

"Ain't that a be-yatch," one began to whine. "A month of the Fish Tank, dawgs. Can you fuckin' believe that? No store, no yard, no weight pile, no nuttin'."

"SHUT THE FUCK UP, YOU FUCKING DEGENERATE! EYES FRONT BEFORE I HAVE YOU SHOT!" yelled the sergeant.

The van went silent and the guard's blood pressure lowered. "Now, most of you ain't real fish," the sergeant continued. "You been down before, so you know what's expected. For those of you dickwads enjoying our hospitality for the first time, you will shower, you will pick up your state issue, and you will receive your cell assignment. Now, OFF THE BUS!!"

As Barry got off the bus another guard grabbed him by his manacles and jacket and threw him against the vehicle. It had to be well over a hundred degrees outside and the side of the bus was scorching hot.

"PUT YOUR HANDS ON YOUR HEADS! NOW!!"

Barry felt a guard unchain and uncuff him and he was then herded with the others in front of a forbidding steel door.

"Lower access!" boomed one of the guards.

The steel door slid open and Barry shuffled into hell. The building had two tiers. There were forty cells per tier arranged in the shape of a horseshoe. There was a staff station on the lower tier and a Plexiglassed gun station on the upper. A large communal shower stall was situated opposite the lower guard station. It was about twenty degrees hotter in there than outside and the entire place smelled of sweat, urine, and fear. From the gun station above Barry heard an authoritative voice boom, "YOU! GET BEHIND THE RED LINE!"

Barry looked up. A shotgun waggled down at him.

"THAT'S RIGHT! YOU! NOW!"

Barry looked down and saw a thick, red line he had inadvertently stepped over. He quickly dragged his toes a full foot behind it.

"NOW STRIP! ALL OF YOU!"

Barry took off what had been, in a different lifetime, his one good suit. He removed his shirt, his shoes, and his socks. Seeing that his neighbor had removed his briefs, Barry took off his shorts, too, and clutched his clothing protectively against his body. It was at this point that he became aware of the noise emanating from behind some of the cell doors.

"Hey, bitch, you wanna come to a party? It's being held in your ass."

"Bend over and say hello, dawg!"

Barry looked up and around him. He could see excited

faces smudged against the postcard windows of cell doors, all enjoying the cabaret of eight naked, sweating new fish. He looked over at the Nazi and saw that his chest contained a mural of a topless woman carrying a spear astride a motorcycle. Barry quickly averted his eyes as he felt the Nazi's head turning toward him once again.

The intake sergeant positioned himself and his clipboard behind a table set up between the men and the shower stall. Eight identical cardboard boxes lay on top of the table.

"Remove all personal items, including jewelry, and add them to your sorry-ass pile of shit," the sergeant ordered.

Barry's only personal item was a wallet containing ten bucks. He removed it from his jacket pocket.

"Two at a time, you fish are gonna step up to the table, put your clothes and effects in the plastic bag provided, making sure to mark your name and list of contents clearly on front of said bag, then pick up one towel, one bar of soap, one bottle of lice-killer shampoo, and proceed to the shower."

Barry did as he was ordered. The shower produced only cold water and the disinfectant masquerading as shampoo burned his eyes and skin. The faces at the cell doors kept up their chatter.

"There's gonna be a part-tay in yo butt tonight, muthafucker."

"And in yo mouth!"

"And all yo friends is comin'!"

After the shower, Barry received an orange jumpsuit and shoes and was duly processed by a convict clerk positioned on the upper tier.

"Profession?"

"Magician."

The clerk smirked. "Well, let's hope you can magic us all the fuck outta here. Cell eighteen, lower tier, lower bunk."

"Thanks, dude."

To Barry's infinite relief, the humorous black guy he had taken a liking to on the bus was assigned to cell eighteen's upper bunk.

"They call me Klepto, dawg."

"Barry."

"Good to meetcha. Sorry it's gotta be in here."

"I hear ya, dawg," said Barry, attempting to fit in.

"You a virgin?"

"What?"

"Is this your first time in the joint?" Klepto asked patiently.

"Yes, it is," Barry admitted.

"Klepto's gonna take care of you, dawg. Soon as you give up the lower bunk."

Barry was indifferent to which three-inch vinyl pallet was his, so he happily switched bunks with his cellmate.

"'Preciate it, Barry," said Klepto, flopping down on the bunk. "But if anyone else asks you to do them a favor, refuse unless there's something in it for you. That's lesson two, dawg."

"What's lesson one?"

"Don't stare at some big Caucasian hoodlum who will fuck you up soon as look at you. I saved your ass on that bus by turning the conversation."

"I know. I appreciate it."

"You're welcome, cellie. Now let's get some fuckin' rest and start doin' this time. Today was a muthafucker, know what I'm sayin', dawg?"

"Yes, I do," said Barry, lying on the steel tray of the upper bunk and looking up at the decaying ceiling.

After a momentary pause, Barry spoke.

"Klepto, what's a 'PV'?"

"Why?"

"You said you were doing a nickel for a PV."

"I'm doing five years for a parole violation. And never ask people what they're in for. That's lesson three. Now get some mothafuckin' sleep."

Somehow, Barry did.

# TWELVE

With no job offer on the horizon, Allie rethought her position on the sex industry. She had spent her life following the rules, and where had it gotten her? Broke, miserable, and accused of a crime she hadn't committed. Maybe it was time to bend the rules. She'd read about a woman who'd stripped so she could afford to buy her brother a motorized wheelchair. Maybe Allie needed to rethink her thinking. It was all about the end justifying the means. If stripping would get her and Barry's lives back on track, then she would strip. Or at least she would keep an open mind. Allie had never even been to a strip club. Angela was right; it was a huge part of the Las Vegas scene, and she owed it to herself to check it out.

On Tuesday nights single women were admitted to Leopards for free. Today was Tuesday.

"Welcome to Leopards, miss," said a liveried doorman, as if welcoming her to the White House or Buckingham Palace rather than a strip joint.

Allie noticed that the entrance to the club was fashioned like an enormous leopard's head. She moved forward and entered the faux feline mouth, treading on the red-carpet tongue. The lobby, lit with subdued blue light, contained a merchandise area, a cloakroom, and the entrance to the main room. Allie decided to pass on purchasing an ashtray in the shape of female genitalia and headed instead straight toward the music.

She spotted Angela almost immediately. She was standing by the bar talking to an enormous man with no neck wearing a tuxedo. Angela herself wore a transparent, halter-topped evening gown, no bra, a thong, and high heels that made her six inches taller. She waved excitedly at Allie and beckoned her over.

"Allie! You came!" said Angela, kissing her on the cheek. "This is Bruno, my favorite security guy."

"Welcome to Leopards, Allie," said Bruno, reciting the club mantra.

"I've got a customer to see to," said Angela. "Bruno will get you a drink on my tab. I'll be back."

Allie watched Angela disappear to a back corner of the room that was even more dimly lit than the rest of the club. There a man nursed a beer, sitting uncomfortably in a comfortable chair. Allie watched Angela lean down to whisper something in his ear. She then reached back behind her neck and unhooked a fastening. In one move the dress Angela was hardly wearing fell off. She hooked one leg over the man's knees and straddled him. Then she began to slowly dance to the beat of the music, her hands wandering over the man's chest and thighs as her naked breasts smacked against his face. The man kept his hands locked rigidly to his side. He looked miserable. More embarrassed for the man than for Angela, Allie averted her eyes. She looked instead at what was happening on the main stage. There, a topless woman sat on the floor with her legs wide open. A portly man in a Tommy Bahama shirt was tucking money into the girl's G-string as she jiggled rhythmically to the music. More banknotes lay on the floor around her, deposited by appreciative patrons. Elsewhere in the club, Allie saw, beautiful women in various states of undress were draped over middle-aged men in various states of excitement. Atop two raised platforms, topless go-go dancers twirled and shimmied. Angela had told the truth; the floors to these ministages were transparent, and a handful of men stood underneath each one, looking upward. Their expressions and the angle of their heads made them look like mechanics appreciating the undercarriage of a particularly fine car.

"Would you like a drink, Allie?" Bruno asked.

"Oh, most definitely," said a wide-eyed Allie. "Vodka and vodka, please."

Bruno tried to make small talk. "How long have you and Summer been seeing each other?" he asked.

"Who's Summer?"

"Summer," said Bruno, gesturing toward Angela.

"Oh," Allie laughed. " 'Summer.' Sorry, what was your question?"

"How long have you two been dating?"

"We're not dating!" said a shocked Allie. "We're just friends."

"Oh. Sorry. I just thought . . . ," said Bruno sheepishly.

"Well, you thought wrong."

"Right."

So Angela was gay. Of course she was. Allie had read somewhere that 90 percent of exotic dancers were at the very least bisexual. It made total sense to her that women who liked women would be attracted to this profession.

Her vodka and vodka was nearly finished when Angela returned.

"Sorry about that, but he was a live one."

Angela held up a bundle of notes. "Three hundred bucks for a ten minute dance . . . I might as well have picked his pocket, he was so helpless."

"Who was he?"

"Conventioneer from South Carolina . . . probably never been to a strip club in his life."

Three hundred dollars for ten minutes worked out to eighteen hundred dollars an hour. Allie was impressed. Just then, a well-groomed man wearing an expensive suit but too much cologne glided up to them. "Hi, Summer. Who's your beautiful friend?"

"Hi, Gordon. This is Allie Bowen. Allie, this is Gordon Sinclair. He owns the joint."

"So, Allie, are you interested in getting up there?" Gordon asked with a mischievous grin.

And there it was. The opportunity to make the sort of money she needed to make. She should say yes.

"I couldn't," Allie heard herself admit. "I'm not tough enough. I just couldn't do it."

"Too bad. A woman as sexy as you could make a bundle."

"I *am* looking for a job, but I couldn't do this."

"Too bad again."

"Are you still looking for a bartender?" asked Angela. "Allie used to work at Heaven."

"Really?" said Gordon. "In the Seraphim bar?"

"Yes," said Angela quickly, before Allie could disagree.

"Well, I am looking for a new bartender. Janne's moving back to Norway to get married."

Allie looked behind her and noticed the blonde Nordic beauty serving drinks. She was relieved to see the woman was fully clothed.

"I'm your gal, Gordon," said Allie. "I'm reliable and conscientious and honest."

"Hey, anyone who uses the word 'conscientious' at least deserves a tryout," said Gordon, smiling. "Come by on Monday, beautiful, and we'll see how you do."

"I will," said Allie, acutely aware that she had only six days to learn how to mix drinks.

✳

The intake processing phase that was supposed to take a maximum of a month had been stretched to forty days of permanent lockdown with no access to either fresh air or exercise.

Inmates were allowed out of their cells for ten minutes every other evening after dinner to take a shower or to line up to use one of the two phones located in the bottom of the cellblock. Barry quickly realized that in ten minutes a prisoner could either make a phone call or take a shower, but accomplishing both tasks during that brief window of opportunity was impossible. Since the temperature in his cell had yet to drop below a hundred degrees, even at night, the choice of a cool shower had always won over Barry's desire to try to call Allie. However, on this particular evening, the fortieth of his incarceration, Barry decided to try for the phone and asked Klepto for advice.

"Lesson twenty-three," said Klepto, lying on his crib. "How to make a phone call."

Klepto had been keeping an accurate tally of all the tips and pointers he had given Barry about prison life. Barry had learned that among convicts the crimes committed commanded different levels of respect. Murder one was considered the most honorable crime; after that came assault, armed robbery, and kidnapping. Most of the inmates in this particular facility were in for some sort of drug charge. Barry's supposed counterfeiting offense was a neutral crime that bordered on cool. Had Barry capped a police officer while resisting arrest, his status would have been much higher; the downside of this being so would his sentence.

Sex crimes were the offenses most frowned upon by

other convicts, and crimes against children were viewed as particularly heinous. Chomos and rapos, as prisoners referred to child molesters and rapists, were often accorded a prison justice far swifter and more violent than any available to a sentencing judiciary. It struck Barry as ironic that sodomizing a rapist was regarded as fit and appropriate punishment, but then he was quickly learning that jailhouse logic was more often than not entirely illogical.

Other advice Klepto had imparted included looking poor, never gambling, buying cigarettes even if you don't smoke, never loaning anything, trying not to make eye contact with anyone, making friends carefully, minding your own business, never snitching, and being as ugly as possible at all times.

"Here's what you do, dawg, to make a call," Klepto told him. "First, you shower in the sink. Ain't no time to shower and phone, know what I'm saying? Then the second the door to our crib cracks open, you run like a muthafucka down those stairs and grab the phone. And if some other muthafucka tries to make you give it up, you stick 'im, unnerstan'?"

Klepto jumped up and waggled the toothbrush that Barry had watched him sharpen against the rough surface of their bare concrete floor. "That's called a shank, dawg. You can borrow it."

"Let me get this right, dude," said Barry. "In order to make a phone call I have to be prepared to commit murder?"

"It's about respect, dawg. Telling people you ain't to be fucked with."

"Hey, I appreciate the advice, Klepto," said Barry with a grin. "But I'm not really into stabbing."

"OK, Barry," sighed Klepto," "You do it your own fucked-up fishy way. My bet is you'll get to talk to your girl for the first time a coupla days before you get outta here."

"She isn't my girl," corrected Barry.

"Well, excuse fucking me," said Klepto.

The cell door popped open and Barry leaped toward it. His footsteps clattered down the steel stairwell and his hand reached for and grasped the nearest phone receiver. That's when he felt a sharp pain at his waist and five large fingers around his throat. The fingers belonged to Idaho, Barry's Nazi nemesis, whom he had inadvertently argued with that first day on the bus. Barry doubted the man had been christened Idaho, but then nobody in this prison society seemed to use the name their parents had given them.

"Unless you want me to stick this shank through your ribs, you'd better give that up, punk," Idaho spat into his ear.

Barry looked down and saw a sharpened Bic pen pressing against his side.

"Fine," said Barry, relinquishing his position at the phone. "My call wasn't urgent."

"Punk bitch," Idaho sneered at him. "I should stick you just for the hell of it."

"Mellow out, dude," said Barry. "Jesus!"

"Get out of my fucking way," said Idaho, pushing Barry aside. "I gotta call my bitch."

Later, back in the cell, Klepto, who had leaned over the

catwalk to watch the scene unfold, shook his head in disgust at Barry's ineptitude.

"When we get moved to gen pop, you're gonna have to take care of bidness, know what I'm saying?"

"Not really," said Barry.

"That crazy shit Idaho is gonna make your life a living hell, 'specially when he gets together with all his peckerwood friends in the yard. You're gonna have to take care of bidness else they gonna fuck with you. That's lesson twenty-four."

Before Barry could learn how he was expected to take care of bidness, the cell door opened and Sergeant Collins, Barry's least favorite prison officer, entered the cell.

"Prisoner nine-six-four-seven-two," Collins barked, meaning Barry. "Come with me."

"Wassup, dawg?" asked Klepto.

"None of your fucking business, Klepto, you stanky, thieving, ignorant, disrespecting motherfucker," said Collins.

Sergeant Collins was having a bad day.

"Fuck, dawg! That is off the hook outta line!" protested Klepto with some justification.

"Keep your bitch yap shut or I'll shut it for you," warned Collins, closing the cell door with a violent thunk that firmly sealed Klepto on one side and Barry and the officer on the other.

Out on the steel catwalk, Barry was commanded to strip. He was surprised at how swiftly he had learned to anesthetize himself from the indignity of a strip search and cavity check. It was one of the horrors that had most frightened him prior to his arrival in prison, but now, faced with the reality, he realized the pointless exercise was just as unpleasant for the police officers as for the prisoners. Barry had come to appreciate that almost every aspect of incarceration was centered around underscoring the entire loss of personal control and power that had been inflicted on the convicted. As a free man, Barry had for years felt an utter lack of control and powerlessness over his life, so the experience of being institutionalized was all going slightly better than he had previously anticipated.

"Warden wants to see you," said Collins contemptuously as he handcuffed Barry and marched him out of the cellblock and across the prison yard.

It had been a boiling hot August day and the sun had not yet set. Barry estimated it was about seven in the evening, and the main yard was still bustling with self-segregating prisoners ethnically grouped in clusters. Lockdown would not happen for at least another hour. Barry spotted the bare-chested skinheads heaving weights over at the weight pile. He also saw a gaggle of Latino inmates collected by the main gate, as though proximity to the gate would somehow hurry their release. After the claustrophobia of the fish tank, the yard felt immense, although in reality the rectangle of dirt that the four cellblocks fed into was probably not even as large as a high school football field. Barry looked up and saw the concrete gun towers at each corner of the perimeter. He estimated it would take about a minute for spraying bullets to assassinate all the inmates below. Two razor-wire-topped fences surrounded the compound, with a six-foot space of no-man's-land separating them. Beyond the second fence stretched a vista of sparsely vegetated desert, interrupted occasionally by a wind funnel of blowing sand.

A new fish being walked across the yard was an event, and dozens of inmates were soon gathered around the duo, accompanying them on their journey. Barry noticed that the dress code seemed more relaxed out here. The state-issued blue denim jeans appeared mandatory, but in many cases the regulation blue work shirts had been replaced by T-shirts and bare chests.

"Wassup, dawg?" someone shouted.

"Same ol' same ol'," responded Barry, delivering the mantra he had heard Klepto employ.

"You good, dawg?" an older voice inquired paternally.

"I'm aigghht," assured Barry.

Barry had spent much time trying to conquer this particular pronunciation and was delighted to have occasion to use it. He had driven his cellie to distraction with his feeble white-boy attempts at this street vernacular version of "all right," and it was only when Klepto tipped him off that the word rhymed with "tight" that he finally mastered it.

"Keep walking," ordered Collins, prodding Barry forward.

They were halfway across the dusty yard now, just passing the prison industry buildings and the chow hall. The cafeteria odor of stale milk, mystery meat, and overcooked vegetables reminded Barry of school days. They passed the chapel, on their way toward the main administrative offices. Barry could taste the grit of sand in his mouth and feel the heat of the still-powerful sun on the back of his unprotected neck.

"Yo, Collins!" a voice shouted. "Wanna smell yo wife's pussy?"

Barry felt Collins momentarily tense behind him.

"Then suck my dick."

Gales of laughter filled the compound. Collins chose to ignore the insult, knowing that any attempt to identify the deliverer of the coarse witticism would prove futile.

"That's harsh," said Barry sympathetically.

"Shut it," said the officer, giving Barry another hard push forward onto an asphalt path that led to the two-story administrative wing.

Inside the building, Barry was shoved down onto a bench outside the warden's office and roughly uncuffed.

"Wait here," ordered Collins.

Ten minutes later, they were summoned into the warden's office.

"Sit down, Morris," said Warden Howard Bain, using Barry's real surname. "Collins, please wait outside."

A low peep of protest escaped Sergeant Collins's lips as he turned and removed himself from the room. A noise sommelier could probably recognize the flavors of disdain, contempt, anger, and a hint of disbelief within the officer's emanation. The warden chose to ignore this and instead gestured Barry to the chair facing his desk. "Sit. Please."

Barry sank into the chair. It was the first comfortable thing he had sat on for two months. He watched as the warden read through the file sitting on his blotter.

"First offense."

Even though the warden's pronouncement was a statement rather than a question, Barry chose to speak.

"Yes, sir."

The warden pulled open a drawer in his desk and removed something from it. He then got up and walked around to face Barry.

"Pick a card."

The warden had fanned a deck of cards open in front of prisoner number 96472.

"What?" asked a confused Barry.

"Pick a card," the warden repeated.

Barry wondered if this was a particularly haphazard form of potluck parole and picked the card the warden was obviously forcing on him.

Warden Howard Bain's résumé made prominent mention of his sociology degree from UNLV, his campaign work for Walter Mondale's failed presidential bid, his early work for the U.S. Department of Justice, and his last fifteen years spent working within the Nevada Department of Prisons. It failed, however, to mention his extracurricular interest in misdirection and sleight of hand.

Inspired by an early encounter at a birthday party almost fifty years ago, Warden Bain had developed a lifelong fascination with magic and magicians. Although just an amateur, he was gifted nonetheless and could always be counted on to perform a few tricks at a social occasion with very little prompting. So the jacket of Barry Morris, aka Barry Houdini, had piqued the warden's interest. Harry Houdini was one of the warden's idols and he owned several books about the man. They were housed within the extensive library that occupied one entire wall of his office.

"Ten of clubs."

"Bull's-eye," said Barry, holding up the card.

"Did you feel me forcing the card?" the warden asked. "Be honest now."

Barry didn't want to hurt the warden's feelings, but he also knew the warden had to be aware that Barry was a professional magician.

"Just a little, but you did it good," Barry lied. "I can show you a way that disguises it completely."

"Just what I was hoping for," said the warden happily. "Morris, this is your lucky day."

"I'm due one, dude."

"I'm sure you are," agreed Warden Bain, who proceeded to make Barry an offer he couldn't refuse.

Barry returned to his cell one hour later with exciting news. In exchange for daily magic lessons, the warden was transferring Barry to general population first thing in the morning. Barry would be working an easy detail in the law library, plus the warden was going to let him borrow any book he wished to read from his extensive collection. Best news of all, the warden had agreed to let Klepto accompany him.

"You da bomb, dawg," said Klepto gratefully. "This is wicked."

In actual fact, it was slightly less wicked than it first appeared, since all the residents of the fish tank were released into general population over the next ten days. However, Barry was grateful for the cushy assignment in the law library that allowed him to read the warden's sizable collection of books on magic for most of the day, as well as for his accommodation in a medium-sized dormitory that slept only eight. Most exciting of all, Barry received forty letters from Allie on his arrival in his new crib and every day brought a new missive from her for him to pore over.

He wrote to Allie that first night and told her he would like to see her, reversing a previous decision he had made to not have her visit him at all during his incarceration. Instead, he told her how she was the one treasured item he missed most of all from the outside world and that seeing her would give him the strength he needed to stay in this human junkyard until he was paroled. He also asked her to bring him a carton of cigarettes, which Allie found perplexing: Barry didn't smoke.

# THIRTEEN

The diploma Allie had earned from a weekend-long intense course in mixology proved unnecessary; most people at Leopards ordered beer. Despite that, Allie did find her new job to be more lucrative than she'd expected. For the first time in her Nevada existence, she had hooked into the economic lifeblood of the Las Vegas service industry: tipping. If Vegas is anything, it is the land of the toke, and Allie found the combination of a cordial personality and a low-cut blouse had a sizable effect on the amount of money she took home at the end of her evening shift.

The club was a petri dish of human behavior. Single guys who came in were usually lonely or curious or both. Groups were traditionally boisterous and noisy as schoolboys, each urging one another on to commit behavior that outside of this joint they would feel awkward indulging in. Allie felt the name of the club was appropriate; there was a definite sense of the hunter and the hunted. What surprised her was that the hunters were the topless females; the hunted were the men.

There was a predatory quality to absolutely every woman who worked in Leopards. Each would scan the crowd for eye contact or a moment of body language that would denote someone susceptible. Once a victim had been targeted, the woman would move in for the kill. "Would you like to dance?" "Where are you from?" "What's your name?" It was all an elaborate con game designed to hustle a guy back into the VIP room. The chief weapons of the huntresses were their (usually) augmented breasts and their ability to stroke the ego of anyone prepared to pay five bucks a minute for the privilege of feeling special. It was immaterial whether a guy was fat, short, skinny, hairy, bald, tall, or sober, or had a body covered in large, red welts oozing green slime. As long as his wallet stayed open, a dancer would happily make him feel as if he were the only man in the world for her.

Allie enjoyed the camaraderie within the club, and soon made friendships with several of the women working there. Curious, one night she asked April, a beautiful Hawaiian-Japanese girl, what exactly transpired back in the VIP room.

"Nothing, honey," giggled April. "That's the scam. All they're buying is a bit more privacy. But they still can only look and not touch."

Allie had a feeling that a few of the girls, including Angela, were prepared to loosen this rule. There was more than one occasion when she had seen her friend leave the club with a customer.

"Hey, what girls do when they leave the club is their business," explained April. "It's not my thing, but some girls don't have a problem with that. That's where the big money is, I guess. Me, I'm saving up to buy a hair salon back home in Oahu and jiggling my boobies is all I need to do to get it."

"Are those real?" asked Allie, gesturing at April's voluminous breasts spilling over her D cups.

"Please," said April dismissively. "I've had them done twice. Bigger tits mean bigger tips, honey. Hey, good looking, wanna dance?"

An attractive, well-built man in his thirties had approached the bar.

"Maybe later. Actually, it was her I wanted to talk to," he said, meaning Allie.

"Bye, sugar," said April, vanishing into the darkness.

"Remember me?" the man asked.

The guy had been into the club five times in the last month and had hit on Allie during each visit. She supposed that there was something about being the only woman in the club who was actually dressed that made her additionally unattainable and therefore additionally desirable.

"Of course," said Allie sweetly. "Jack Daniel's on the rocks?"

"You got it. So, you thought about my offer?"

The last time the man had been in the club he had offered Allie a thousand dollars if she would get up on stage and strip.

"It's never off my mind," said Allie facetiously.

"And . . . ?"

"Not for one million dollars," she replied, handing him his drink.

He shook his head.

"Man, you're driving me crazy."

"Glad I could oblige."

"My name's Tim, by the way."

"Allie."

"I know. I asked," he said, leaving a twenty-dollar bill on the bar and the scent of expensive cologne in the air. He walked down to a table in the club and took a seat a discreet distance from the stage just as Angela hurried up to the bar.

"Do you wanna earn an extra five hundred bucks tomorrow night?" she asked furtively.

Allie looked at her suspiciously. "What do I have to do?"

"Absolutely nothing. I'll explain after work."

Later, over a wind-down drink at a local bar, Angela explained to Allie what she would have to do to earn the five hundred dollars.

"Katrina and I have been doing some tricks on the side," Angela admitted. "It's serious money; we've been getting two grand a time. The guys who can pay that sort of money are much classier than the scumbags you meet at Leopards."

Allie failed to believe that men who paid for sex were classy in any way whatsoever, nor did she believe all the customers who visited the club were entirely scummy, but she let both points slide.

"We've been working for this escort service, but we want to cut them out. That's where you come in."

"What would I have to do?" Allie asked as she signaled for another round of drinks.

"We've got this one regular guy. Katrina gave him her home number. We've done him before. He likes us to—"

"I don't need to know the gory details," interrupted Allie. "Again, what would I have to do?"

"You sit in the casino bar. If we're not down from the room in thirty minutes, you call security and say you heard a commotion as you walked past the room. Give them the room number. That's it."

"That's it?"

"Totally."

After her rent, gas, and general living expenses, Allie had managed to save just over a thousand dollars in six weeks. She realized she had to give serious consideration to any acceptable means of augmenting her income. Sitting in a bar with a cell phone for half an hour did not sound that trying.

So the next night Allie sat in the bar at one of the Strip's swankier casinos and sipped a piña colada. She tried to look nonchalant, but her heart was doing the merengue. Any moment, Allie expected the police to enter the bar and arrest her. Wasn't the bartender giving her a strange look? He was no doubt only seconds away from reaching for the phone to report her behavior as suspicious. And what was happening upstairs? They were both probably dead.

Her drink was only half-finished when Allie looked up to see Angela and Katrina hurrying toward her.

"What's happened? What went wrong?" Allie asked, panicked.

"Nothing," said Angela. "We're done."

Allie looked at her watch. She'd only been there for fifteen minutes.

"But . . ."

"I told you it was an easy gig," Angela interrupted.

Angela paid Allie her five hundred dollars as the trio waited to claim their cars from the valet. Fifteen minutes later, Allie was back in her apartment. She was too wired to sleep. She couldn't believe how easily the night had gone. There was an opportunity here, if only she could think of the right angle.

Allie acted as the girls' personal alarm system on two more occasions before driving out two hundred miles into the desert to visit the ex-husband she had landed in jail. Parking her car, Allie could clearly see the coils of razor wire that surrounded the compound, and it was with enormous trepidation and a bone-dry mouth that she boarded the bus that transported her and the other visitors up to the main gate.

Once inside the cramped waiting room, Allie was

handed a pamphlet to peruse entitled *Rules for Visitors of the Nevada Prison System.* She was amused and slightly horrified to see the dress code for female visitors warned, "You must wear underwear."

After a twenty-minute wait, the visitors were ushered one by one through a metal detector and into a small cafeteria containing a few vending machines and lots of tables. Allie spotted Barry immediately and promptly burst into tears.

"I look that bad, then, do I?" he asked as she sat down.

"No, no," she sniffled. "Actually you look really good."

It was true. Barry had been spending a lot of time at the weight pile. His body now had a far more chiseled definition and his face had a leaner, older look that suited him.

"Then why are you crying?"

"I'm just really happy to see you, Barry," she said, leaning over the table to kiss him on the cheek.

She looked up to see a sign posted prominently behind Barry's head: PROLONGED KISSING WILL RESULT IN IMMEDIATE TERMINATION OF THE VISIT.

Allie sat down quickly, not wanting to be responsible for getting Barry into further trouble. "You're getting my letters, then?" she asked.

"They're really helping me get through this," said Barry.

"Is the warden still helping you?"

Barry had written to Allie to tell her about his good fortune regarding Warden Bain. "Yes. He's still letting me use his personal library. I'm learning so much in here, Allie."

Allie didn't want to dwell on what Barry might be learning in prison. "That's great," she said. "I've got three thousand dollars saved up already, Barry. By the time you get out, I might be able to get twenty put away."

Barry pursed his lips and looked away.

"What's wrong?" asked Allie.

"Nothing. That's fantastic."

"Barry, it's me. What's wrong?"

"I need two hundred thousand," Barry blurted out, shocking them both.

"What?"

And the plan Barry had been bursting to tell her poured out of him. "I've been studying all of the warden's books, particularly the ones about Houdini," he said. "You were right, Allie. I am a good magician, and I just needed to get focused. This experience has focused me. We can make a great business partnership, Allie. Your PR ability and my wacky ideas can catapult us to the top."

Leaving aside the fact that Barry had asked her to raise two hundred thousand dollars, Allie was excited at Barry's excitement. She hadn't seen him like this for years. Correction, she hadn't seen him like this ever. She was determined not to deflate his enthusiasm, but she also needed to bring him back down to earth.

"Explain the two hundred thousand dollars part to me again," she asked.

"I am designing so many cool tricks in here. Little spins on old tricks I've found in these books and entirely new things that just come to me in the middle of the night. But we're gonna need some up-front financing. Do you think your parents could help?"

Allie had yet to tell her parents that she no longer worked at Heaven. She had sent them a Christmas card, but she didn't think that would persuade them to sell their house to help Barry's career.

"I don't think that'll work," said Allie.

"But can you do it, Allie? Can you raise that sort of money? I'm counting on you."

Allie searched for the phrase that would neither promise nor refuse Barry's request.

"I'll do my absolute best."

"That's my girl."

"THAT'S IT," a guard announced loudly. "SAY YOUR GOOD-BYES."

"I can't believe that was all our time," Allie said incredulously. "I haven't asked you half the things I wanted to ask."

Barry shrugged. "Life in here sucks, and I miss you like crazy," he said. "What else did you want to know?"

"I guess that just about covers it," said Allie. "I'd better not kiss you good-bye. I don't want to get you in trouble."

"Trouble's my middle name," said Barry, leaning over the table and kissing her passionately on the mouth.

"Bye, babe," said Barry and he was gone.

"B . . . bye," stammered Allie, surprised by the passion of the kiss and finding herself strangely drawn to this improved version of her ex-husband.

On her way back to her car, she made sure to look on the ground in case someone had dropped two hundred thousand dollars. She found nothing. Never mind. Barry's enthusiasm had emboldened her. If he could be optimistic about turning his life around, then why couldn't she? Maybe together she and Barry could even pay back that son of a bitch Christian Sacco.

# FOURTEEN

Christian Sacco, the supreme object of Allie's disaffection, was at that moment in an open canoe fifty miles outside of Bangkok. Sitting with his Bruno Magli's crunched under Richard Summerford's butt, Christian was watching Wishan, their Thai guide, search for the concealed entrance to an exclusive restaurant that promised illicit culinary delights. The restaurant that Summerford hoped to lure to Heaven would hopefully also bring them shelter from the tropical rain that was now pounding into the boat in drops the size of dinner plates.

Christian had been in a foul mood since arriving in Thailand. The flight from Las Vegas with Richard had not gone well. Richard had confided to Christian that, once the Hello Good-bye project (as the hotel's top secret maternity and funeral idea had been nicknamed) was up and running, he had all but been assured he would be kicked upstairs to the parent company's board of directors. However, despite Christian's several transpacific attempts to make Richard promise to recommend him as his successor, no such commitment had been forthcoming. Indeed, Christian got the distinct impression that Summerford favored the toadying and pedestrian Frank DiPaulo as Heaven's next president. That made sense. Christian was a comer who might overshadow his predecessor's reign. There was a possibility that Christian might improve Heaven and that was the last thing Richard needed. A phrase Richard never wanted to hear was "You know, Heaven's profits have doubled since Summerford left."

On the chessboard of office politics, Christian was temporarily in check. He was going to need a bold move to get himself out of that position.

"Over there, Mr. Richard," said Wishan, gesturing with his chin toward the riverbank. As he paddled through the caramel water, a smiling Thai beauty suddenly appeared, stepping from behind the thick green foliage to help Wishan tie the craft to the restaurant's wooden dock.

"Welcome to Phranga restaurant," she announced with a wide grin and a traditional wai greeting, pressing her palms together and raising them in front of her spectacularly beautiful face. "My name is Janjira. Please follow. My father is waiting."

The men followed obediently, their eyes fixed on Janjira's playful bottom. Christian turned to see their river navigator waving good-bye from his peeling wooden boat. He noticed Wishan was smiling broadly as well. At first, Christian had enjoyed the genial disposition that all Thai people seemed to possess, but now he was becoming suspicious. *How could anyone whose job it is to row people across shit-colored water in a fucked-up canoe be that happy?* he thought. *Are these people on drugs?*

His favorite smiling person so far had been the man who had accosted them outside their hotel as they hurried to their river rendezvous.

"You want fuck? You want live pussy show? You want girl to sucky-sucky?" the man had inquired with the politeness of an English butler offering a pot of tea.

Christian was beginning to think everyone in this country was playing an angle. Surely the entire population couldn't be as sociable and happy as it appeared?

"These people are creeping me out," Christian now complained to Richard.

"It's called 'the Land of Smiles' for a reason," Richard retorted as Janjira motioned them toward a waiting tuk-tuk.

Christian and Richard climbed into the rear seats as Janjira slid into the driver's position. The rickety vehicle had more in common with a motorbike than a car, and Janjira was evidently not on a list of the ten most careful drivers in Thailand. She steered the tuk-tuk down the steep hill, narrowly missing trees as Richard and Christian hung tightly on to the sides of the vehicle, which finally came to a rest in a forest clearing a few hundred yards from the riverbank.

"Welcome to Phranga restaurant," Janjira announced again. "You bite the snake before it bites you. That is our slogan. Catchy, huh?"

"Catchy . . . yes," Richard replied, looking around his feet for snakes.

They were standing in front of a collection of wooden huts raised high above the jungle floor by thick bamboo posts. Each structure had a uniquely designed sloped roof with glassless windows decorated with bursts of floral color. Slatted wooden ladders led to teak floor landings full of elegant yet simply dressed dining tables of various dimensions.

"We could build this whole setup near the Sports Book," Richard suggested. "That Irish pub has to go. Everybody and their uncle has one of those. And look at the business this place is doing in the middle of a jungle. In Vegas, we can't even get anyone to go downtown."

It was true the Phranga restaurant was teeming. Every table in every hut was full, and there was a crowd of at least a dozen people standing expectantly at the restaurant's entrance. They were all holding what appeared to be small plastic snakes in their hands.

"Number thirty-one," the smiling hostess called out.

Richard heard a rattle and a gray-haired man held his snake up in the air. "Thirty-one," he said excitedly, walking forward and handing the hostess his plastic snake.

"This is fantastic," Richard crowed. "It's a reptilian Cheesecake Factory."

Christian spotted a table of four male customers, each drinking a large glass of something that looked like ketchup. The care and delight in their consumption suggested the drink was something far more exotic, however.

"Mr. Summerford, I presume?"

Christian turned to see a beaming, older man bowing vigorously at Richard.

"Mr. Phranga. A great joy to meet you."

Christian didn't think it was physically possible, but the man's smile actually widened. *Maybe all those people weren't really smiling,* he thought. *Maybe they were depressed, and this is the first actual smile I've seen.*

Christian was grudgingly impressed as Richard returned the man's gratitude with an unself-consciously performed wai greeting of respect.

"Come. Let me give you—how do you say it?—the stageback tour," Phranga announced conspiratorially. "You bite the snake before the snake bites you. That is our new slogan. Catchy, huh?"

Richard and Christian smiled and followed the man through the restaurant and out to the kitchens. Christian gagged at the smell and the lack of hygiene.

"Come. This way," Phranga gestured.

They jumped over a stream of suspiciously colored running water in the dirt alley behind the kitchen, made their way through a door off that alley, and entered a small courtyard. Christian heard the hissing at once. It was coming from a pit in the far corner of the compound. To their left was a cage containing a small creature Christian had never before seen in his entire life; it looked like a rat, only it was twice as big.

"What the hell is that?" he asked.

"A mongoose," Mr. Phranga replied.

"You eat that?" Christian inquired with horror.

Phranga laughed. "No, no. The mongoose is there to anger the snake. It is his natural enemy, and the cage protects the mongoose and frustrates the snake. The more angry the snake, the stronger its medicinal qualities; the more its blood pumps, the more powerful it becomes."

"What snake?" said Christian, as Phranga picked up a metal stick with a hooked end and used it to undo the entrance to the six-foot-deep hissing pit.

Very carefully, Christian peered inside. There were at least forty to fifty cobras slithering below him; the smallest had to be over six feet long.

"I get you a good one," Phranga promised. "A big, ferocious one."

And with that Phranga used the end of his stick to catch and pull one of the cobras out of the pit and onto the courtyard floor.

Both Christian and Richard momentarily tossed aside their masculinity and fled to the courtyard's farthest corner. Phranga concentrated on avoiding the hissing monster's venomous fangs as he goaded the snake with the mongoose and the stick. He next removed a length of rope from his jacket pocket and successfully looped one end around the head of the furious, twisting creature. He pulled the noose tight, and the snake's mouth widened in a grimace that clearly revealed its deadly fangs. Phranga tied the rope to a hook in the wall and removed a knife from his belt. With the dangling snake still obviously alive, he began to cut the creature wide open from the head to the tail.

"I don't know if there's an animal rights group for snakes," Christian whispered, "but if there is, we're gonna hear from them."

But Richard wasn't listening. He was entranced.

"This is gold," he whispered.

"Come nearer," Phranga told them. "It is harmless now."

They hadn't noticed Janjira's entrance, but she was now in the courtyard, clutching a glass and a small pair of nail scissors. She positioned the glass at the bottom of the snake and collected the snake's dripping blood.

"This is good. Sweet and thick," Phranga murmured approvingly.

"You drink the blood?" asked Christian woozily.

"And the bile," Phranga nodded.

They ventured closer as Phranga stuck his fingers inside the snake and found a small pocket of translucent skin that he now cut away from the body of the reptile.

"The snake's gallbladder contains very powerful gastric juices," he informed them.

He snipped off the end of the skin pocket and poured the contents into the bloody cocktail. "There it is," he announced, handing the glass to Richard. "The appetizer."

Richard took the glass and glanced nervously at Christian.

"Your idea," said Christian. "Bottoms up."

Richard took a swig. To his surprise, the concoction was warm and sweet, and there was a primeval satisfaction to drinking it. He wiped his bloodstained lips with the back of his hand and handed the glass to Christian.

"It's good. Try it."

Christian took the glass and held it to his lips. Richard had drunk it. He had to at least try. "Well, it can't be any worse than my last girlfriend's cooking," he joked.

Christian raised the concoction to his lips and sipped a tiny portion. It was unlike anything he had ever tasted or ever wanted to taste again. "Best snake blood I've ever had. I can actually taste the mongoose's anger," he quipped, quickly handing the glass back to Richard.

Not wanting to bruise a business opportunity by accidentally insulting their host, Richard quickly finished the potion off. "Extraordinary."

Phranga nodded approvingly. "Now we chop the snake meat up and fry it in oil," he announced.

As the two casino executives sat in the restaurant and mulled over what they had seen, Christian decided to try the cooked snake meat. To his surprise, it tasted a lot like chicken.

"It's a winner, Christian," announced Richard. "The Asians will like it and the Americans will think it's unusual and prestigious."

Christian didn't reply. He was too busy chewing on a particularly tough piece of cobra. Richard looked up at the sky.

"It looks like it's going to rain again. Maybe we should say our good-byes and head back to the hotel," he decided.

On the boat trip back to Bangkok, Christian discovered the real reason he had been brought along on the trip.

"We should spend a couple more days here, don't you think?" said Richard casually. "Check out the shows. See if there's anything we could adapt for Vegas' adult appetite. That's your sort of area, yes?"

Richard was a very inexperienced philanderer. It dawned on Christian that Richard wanted him to act as a tour guide to Eastern decadence. Interesting. They were in a land where sex was sold like lemonade, and Richard was a man who had been married to the same woman for over twenty years. Christian's senses began to hum. One slip by Richard and Christian could be out of check.

Christian immediately went in search of the smiling pimp, Naret, who had approached them earlier. For a few thousand bahts Christian received a very thorough précis of the carnal delights the city had to offer. Naret told him about the hairdressing salon where customers could receive both a blow-dry and a blow job. Naret also enthusiastically recommended the club where naked girls write customers' names on parchment using just their swiveling hips and a paintbrush protruding from their genitals. He also insisted Christian not miss the famous all-body massage, in which a lissome, naked Thai goddess would use every inch of her skin to lather her customer to distraction, using the only soap pad with which Mother Nature had endowed her. Christian suspected all of these possibilities might be too down and dirty for Richard Summerford. He decided instead to take his boss to what Naret insisted was the crème de la crème of the go-go clubs in Nana Plaza, the city's most infamous red-light district. The Lollipop Club, Naret swore, contained both the youngest, freshest, sexiest, most innocent girls, straight from the countryside . . . as well as a few surprises.

Later that evening, sweating copiously in the humidity, Christian and Richard navigated the busy streets of Nana Plaza, alternately ogling and avoiding neon-lit nightclubs, massage parlors, bars, pool halls, tuk-tuks, taxis, street stalls, motorbikes, hawkers, and hookers who accosted them on every corner.

"You wanna be my darling all night?"

"Hello, my hansum man. Come inside, please. You be my big, big honey."

"This is it," said Christian, pushing Richard through a

doorway that looked ominously similar to all the other doorways they had passed.

Inside the club, a brightly lit stage jutted into the barely lit auditorium. The men from Heaven were quickly ushered into the heart of the action and seated at the very apex of the thrust stage. Naret apparently had called ahead.

"Can we sit farther back?" Richard pleaded, obviously uncomfortable.

"Best seats in the house," said the club manager. "You special guests. You see later."

"We don't want to offend them," said Christian to Richard, taking his seat in front of the raised stage.

Richard sighed and reluctantly sat, his knees brushing against the black curtain that was fastened along the bottom of the stage and draped down to the floor. He looked up. A couple of chrome poles that reached up to the ceiling broke up the bare staging. Christian sighed. *If you've seen one strip joint, you've seen them all,* he thought, bored already with the monotony of the relentless background music.

Christian ordered two beers and waited for the show to begin as the lights dimmed. Noy, the club's emcee, entered the stage, wearing only black leather boots and a smile.

"How you doing tonight, honeys?" she cheerfully inquired as she produced a bunch of bananas.

Richard leaned over to Christian. "What's she going to do with those?" he inquired.

"I'm not sure, but I think she's going to put them in her—"

"No!" gasped Richard.

"Oh, yes!" said Christian. "There they go. And here they come."

To say Noy had a hidden talent would not do her justice as she launched bananas around the room in perfect syncopation to the music pulsating through the speakers. Her closing trick was particularly impressive. Positioning herself in front of one of the chrome poles, she first grabbed backward, hoisting herself up until her splayed, perpendicular legs were at right angles to the pole. She then raised her bottom even farther into the air and shot a yellow missile forcefully into the balcony. It was the equivalent of a vaginal fireworks display.

"If Vegas ever gets an NBA team," said Christian as he and Richard applauded, "she should give out the free T-shirts at halftime."

Noy was merely an aperitif. Various acts of both simulated and real debauchery followed, each more outrageous than the previous. It was during the final tableau, when six people were undoubtedly having group sex on a turntable bed six feet from where he was sitting, that seen-it-all-before Christian was surprised for the first time that night.

He felt the curtained area below the stage move. The head of a young Thai girl emerged in front of Christian's knees and unzipped his fly. Christian looked across at Richard, who wore an expression of utter amazement as apparently the same thing was happening to him with another girl. Completely unseen by the other members of the audience because of the position of his chair and the darkness of the room, Christian then received the most efficient and satisfying oral treat he had ever been given.

The Thai girl and her mouth retreated below the stage just as the show ended.

"Jesus," said Christian.

"Nnnngagaahhh," said Richard.

Naret bounded up to them just as Christian stuffed himself back into his pants. "You like my VIP present?" Naret laughed.

"It was very thoughtful," said Christian.

"Nnnngggaahhh," said Richard.

"It is the house special," Naret continued with a grin.

"Aaah . . . that's why it's called the Lollipop Club," said Christian.

"Exactly. You bring this show to Las Vegas? Naret come as interpreter, no?"

So that was what was on his scheming little mind, was it? Christian had suspected as much. One whiff of a show like the one he had just seen and the Gaming Commission would take away Heaven's license before a single banana had touched the ground.

"It's a definite possibility," lied Christian.

"Whichever girls you like in show, I get them for you," Naret offered.

"Thank you, but we're here on business," said Christian.

"The girl under the stage," said Richard suddenly. "I want the girl from under the stage."

"Those girls are beginners. Fresh from the country," explained Naret. "Some are even virgins."

"That girl was no beginner," insisted Richard. "I have to meet her."

"I see what I can do," offered Naret, and he retreated backstage.

Christian worried that Richard would be disappointed. He suspected the homelier girls got to work behind the curtain. However, when Naret returned five minutes later, it was with a girl whom Christian honestly believed could have represented Thailand in the Miss Universe pageant.

"This is Somchai. She new. She only been here a week."

Somchai was tall, with ample breasts and limpid brown eyes. Her toffee-colored skin was flawless and her straight, waist-length, jet-black hair glistened under the club's few lights. She appeared shy and demure as she offered Richard a traditional wai greeting. Naret pulled Christian to one side. "He want short or long time?"

Christian looked over at his boss stroking the girl's hair. "Long time, I think," he decided, knowing he would be heading back to the hotel alone.

*Early the next* morning, Christian was woken by his ringing phone.

"It's me," said Summerford. "Come up to my room."

Christian dutifully trotted up to the room and knocked gently on the door. It was opened by Somchai, wearing a fluffy white robe.

"Hi," she whispered.

"Hi," said Christian, amazed all over again at her flawless beauty.

Christian entered the room. Richard was lying naked in bed, a single sheet pulled up to his waist. He looked ten years younger, despite the gray hair that populated his chest. Somchai balanced decorously on the side of the bed, clutching the robe around her throat and looking directly at Christian. Richard extended an arm and stroked her shoulders gently and protectively.

"Christian, I need your help," Summerford announced. "This woman is amazing. Incredible. I want you to hear her story. She speaks good English."

Somchai then began to regale Christian with her tale of woe. She was twenty-one. She had grown up in a village in a family of twelve. A man came to the village over a year ago and promised to make her and her family rich. He paid her family an advance and told her she would be a maid for a wealthy Bangkok family. Instead, he took her to the Lollipop Club. Now she was in debt bondage, and was forced to provide sexual services to customers until the advance, plus exorbitant interest on the advance, was paid back in full.

"Christian, I'm a fifty-five-year-old man. I've been married for twenty-five years. Until last night, I had never been unfaithful to Cindy," Richard explained. "I've decided to take Somchai back to Las Vegas with me. I deserve her. I need her. And I need you to help me."

Christian sat in an armchair next to the oriental armoire that contained a TV set and pondered how best to play out this scenario. "What can I do?" he finally asked.

"Your friend Naret," Richard explained. "He must know the pimp she owes the money to. Pay him off."

"Check."

"And find out who we can bribe to get a passport and a visa."

"That might take a little longer."

"So we'll stay until it gets done. I'm not leaving without her," said Summerford forcefully. "Just get it done."

Somchai snuggled contentedly against Summerford's chest as Christian went in search of Naret. Exporting this piece of tail for Summerford would give Christian enormous leverage. He had to find Naret.

It took Christian most of the morning, but he finally located Naret in a crowded coffee shop just off Nana Plaza. Christian explained the situation. Naret tut-tutted and shook his head slowly from side to side.

"This girl is a liar," Naret announced. "She is a naughty, bad girl."

"What do you mean?" Christian asked, and was thrilled when he heard what Naret had to tell him.

*An hour later,* Christian was back in Richard Summerford's room. The lovers were now dressed. Christian pulled notes from a roll of baht currency and handed them to Somchai.

"Go get a suitcase and some new clothes," he told her.

She kissed Richard tenderly and skipped out of the room, promising to be back by five.

"I never thought I'd ever be with someone as perfect as that," said Richard wistfully as the door gently closed shut.

Christian debated whether to tread softly or be direct. He decided the direct approach would be the most painful to Summerford and the most enjoyable to him.

"She's a guy," said Christian.

For a moment, Christian thought Richard was going to punch him. "Don't be so fucking stupid," he growled. "She's a girl. I've been down there. I know."

"She's what they call a *katoey*. She's had the full nip and tuck. But even without the goods, she's still a he."

"But—"

"That's why their job is to give customers head," Christian continued. "They used to own the equipment, so they know how to handle it."

"I don't believe you," gasped Richard hoarsely.

"She's abnormally tall. Real Thai girls are tiny with little breasts. That's why her tits are so big. They're manufactured."

Christian was reveling in Richard's writhing, emotional discomfort. "Anyone could have made the same mistake," Christian offered. "She's extraordinarily beautiful. I can understand exactly why—"

"Enough," commanded Summerford. "Let's get out of here and on the plane before it comes back."

It was some hours later, somewhere over the Pacific, that Summerford turned to damage control. "Nobody in Las Vegas must ever know anything about this," he said.

Christian remained silent.

"Your silence will not go unrewarded. I will propose you to the board as my successor as president."

"I really appreciate that, Richard," said Christian, allowing himself a small smirk of satisfaction. Checkmate.

# FIFTEEN

Columbus Day weekend was a big weekend everywhere in Las Vegas and Leopards was no exception. Extra dancers were employed, including attractive California coeds from USC and UCLA who flew into town on bargain airline tickets and used the money they earned lap dancing to help pay their tuition. Allie thought she recognized the new dancer who looked like Jennifer Lopez, but couldn't quite place her. It was only when she heard her backstage singing along to Jessica Simpson's latest single that Allie put it all together. That voice was impossible to forget.

"Didn't you used to work in the Seraphim Lounge?" asked Allie.

"Yeah, until some prick called Christian Sacco fired my ass."

Malfi Molini was bitter. Max had broken up with her when he moved back to New Jersey after his divorce. Not surprising, considering the paucity of her talent, without Max's assistance, Malfi had failed to find work anywhere as a singer. Instead, Malfi had found a job working as a greeter in a new high-end restaurant on Sahara Avenue, but the pay was dismal. Stripping, she decided, was the only option that would both elevate her income and satisfy her performing urge.

Allie was impressed at Malfi's enthusiasm and energy on stage. She was certainly a crowd-pleaser and she had the type of terrific, all-natural body that Jennifer Lopez had made fashionable.

"She's pretty, but not as pretty as you," commented a man to Allie as he leaned on the bar.

It was Allie's admirer, Tim, hitting on her again.

"What do I have to do to make you go out with me?" he asked. "I'll give you a thousand dollars for one date. No sex; just dinner and a show."

Allie had been looking for ways to supplement her income since visiting Barry in jail. She had helped organize a couple of bachelor parties starring Angela and a few of the girls from the club. These had proven surprisingly lucrative, but she was still a laughable distance away from the two hundred thousand Barry needed to build his new act. Allie was beginning to feel like she was failing Barry all over again. She wasn't prepared to strip, but she was prepared to do something out of her comfort zone.

"Mister, you've got yourself a date," said Allie, surprising the hell out of Tim. "And I promise the thousand dollars will go toward a very good cause."

They spent the next five minutes running through all the available shows on the Strip. Their choice was narrowed by the fact that Allie had seen most of the big shows with Christian. In the end they decided that *Legends*, the impersonator show at the Imperial Palace, would be a fun date, and Allie agreed to meet Tim at Spago at six p.m. on her day off for a pretheater dinner.

*Fifty miles away*, Barry was having dinner discussions of his own. His day up to that point had gone very well; he was finally happy with a new trick he had developed that would allow him to dangle upside down in a straitjacket above the audience while setting himself on fire. His euphoria, however, was cut short when Idaho appeared at his cafeteria table and stood menacingly over him. "I'm still hungry, bitch. Give me your dinner."

"Hey, dude, I'm hungry, too," said Barry in a tiny voice. "I can't help you out today."

Idaho lowered his oversized cranium so that his mouth was only a few inches from Barry's left ear. "You talkin' out the side of your neck at me, punk?" he spat.

"Dude, leave me the fuck alone, OK?"

All other conversations at the table stopped as everyone focused their attention on Barry's confrontation with Idaho.

"You ever talk to me like that again, needle-dick, and I will fuck you up big-time," threatened Idaho as he picked up Barry's entire tray and swaggered away.

Barry felt transported back to the lowest depths of his miserable school days, when his easygoing affability had made him prey to bullies. He bit his bottom lip hard, stood up, and walked out of the hall.

Hours later, he lay in bed in the dark, still seething. Tonight, for once, the shouts and screams of other prisoners and the clanging of distant steel doors failed to bother him. He had only one thought: Klepto was right. If he was going to live to his parole date, Barry was going to have to take care of business.

He was already aware of the few places that were hidden from the yard's video surveillance or gun towers. Barry lay awake contemplating the various possible permutations and decided that the narrow alley between the weight pile and the fourth cellblock was the optimum location. There, he could meet Idaho and "discuss" how, moving forward, they might mutually coexist in the prison.

Early next morning, Barry removed the batteries from the radio Allie had sent him. He then went down to the prison store to purchase a couple of cans of chili. As he saw Idaho lumber up the alleyway, Barry emerged from the shadows and followed him. Idaho wore no shirt. His back rippled with a full portrait of a motorbike-riding, swastika-wearing Grim Reaper, complete with glowing red eyes. The bony figure was slashing his scythe at a naked, prostrate woman with long dark hair and heavy breasts.

From under his denim jacket, Barry quickly removed the large sock into which he had stuffed the batteries, the cans of chili, and two padlocks Klepto had loaned him. Taking aim, he swung it hard at Idaho's head.

On impact, Idaho visibly sagged. The back of his skull bloomed with blood. As he turned, the second blow connected with his face and broke his nose. The third blow shattered several of his front teeth, but he still kept moving forward. Barry held the sock in both hands and swung it like a baseball bat. It connected to the side of Idaho's head like a hammer hitting an egg. Idaho fell unconscious to the ground, the blood still pouring from his nose and mouth, forming a puddle on the hot asphalt. By now a small crowd of inmates had gathered around and Barry quickly retreated back into the yard. He dropped the batteries, cans, and locks into the dirt and stuffed the bloody sock into a previously reconnoitered hole in the concrete wall at the back of the weight pile.

"MAN DOWN! MAN DOWN!" yelled a pimply faced, panicked officer into his walkie-talkie.

"BACK IN YOUR FUCKING HOUSES," yelled another guard as the alarm sounded.

Barry thrust his still-shaking hands in his pockets and joined the shuffle toward his cellblock. Klepto caught up with him.

"You schlocked him good," Klepto noted approvingly. "You kill him?"

"What? No. I hope not," said Barry.

"Then let's hope you busted his cap good enough for him to stay in the infirmary a long muthafuckin' time," said Klepto.

"I think I did, man," said Barry.

"Good," said Klepto, adding with a smirk, "you some crazy, white boy, know what I'm sayin'?"

Barry smiled. "Hey, Klepto . . . ?"

"Wassup?"

"I took care of my bidness, dawg."

"Mines bidness," corrected Klepto.

✳

*The date with* Tim was not going well. Robbed of the background noise of Leopards, multiple Jack Daniels, and the topic of why Allie refused to go out with him, dinner conversation between the pair was stilted. Allie learned that Tim sold insurance to high-end clients and drove a Porsche. He had been married briefly to a wife who had left him for one of his better customers. Allie was determined to betray none of her own personal details, so her available areas of conversation were by definition limited. Somewhere in the middle of the entrées, it all came to a grinding halt, and they just stared at one another and chewed. Suddenly, Tim's face lit up as he spotted someone he knew entering the restaurant. "There's one of my clients," he told Allie. "This guy has a killer, top-of-the-line Mercedes. I should go say hi."

Tim jumped up and a few minutes later brought over Christian Sacco. A beautiful brunette accessory with lips like air bags clung to Christian's arm.

"Christian Sacco, I'd like you to meet Allie Bowen," said Tim proudly.

"We've met," said Christian. "Still in town, huh, Allie?"

"Sure, she's still in town," said Tim. "She works at Leopards."

Allie died a small death.

"I'll have to come down and stick a dollar in your G-string," said Christian.

"I'm on the management side," Allie retorted, daring Tim with her eyes to contradict her.

"Congratulations on your promotion, Christian," said Tim.

"Thanks."

"Promotion?" asked Allie.

"Oh, haven't you heard?" said Christian. "I've been named the new president of Heaven."

Allie sagged visibly. The fragile universe she was beginning to rebuild for herself had caved in once more. Christian as president of Heaven! There was no justice in the world.

"Can we eat, Chris? I'm famished," moaned the brunette.

"Of course," said Christian. "Good to see you, Allie. You kids have a great evening."

"We're going to see *Legends* at the Imperial Palace," said Tim.

"I guess somebody has to," said Christian, and he and his date made their way to their table.

"Now, what were we talking about?" Tim asked.

"Huh?"

"Before."

Allie racked her brains. "Ummm. You were explaining term life insurance versus whole life insurance. Which did you say was the best?"

"Well, that depends."

And Tim reembarked on a conversation that was duller than watching senior golf in slow motion.

An hour later Allie and Tim were ushered into the showroom of the Imperial Palace, a centrally located but somewhat dilapidated casino and hotel that surprisingly Allie had never been inside before. The *Legends* show of celebrity impersonators was energetic and affable; Allie soon fell into the show's well-crafted trap of making the audience believe they were seeing the original artists rather than mere copies. She was amazed at how easy it was for her and the rest of the audience to suspend their disbelief as pretend pop icons followed one another. The faux Celine Dion received just as rapturous an applause as the real Celine Dion received across the street at Caesars. And the Britney Spears look-alike was every bit as sexy as the real Britney Spears.

"Aannngghhh!" yelped Allie, excitedly. *That's it! That's it!* People turned in their seats to check where the noise had come from.

"Are you all right?" whispered Tim worriedly.

"I'm fine," said Allie.

"You made a very strange noise."

"Did I? Sorry."

But she wasn't sorry; she was ecstatic. The Britney Spears impersonator had given her a business idea of such force and clarity that it had inspired an involuntary yelp. Allie's brain raced. Could such a concept really work? If it did, was it something that could give Barry the money he needed? What was the downside? Well, it was probably illegal, and she'd promised herself she'd only bend life's rules, not flout them. However, Christian had flouted the rules and it had gotten him the dream job he had always coveted. She needed to go somewhere quiet to think this thing through. As soon as the show ended, she told Tim she needed to be up early the next day and should be getting home.

Tim had already accepted that the date had not gone well. Allie seemed much more fun at Leopards; he couldn't believe she'd made him talk about life insurance for twenty minutes. Twice. Happy to bring the date to an end, he pulled ten one-hundred-dollar bills out of his wallet as they waited in the taxi line outside the casino.

"A deal's a deal," he said despondently, offering the cash to Allie.

"Forget it," replied Allie as she got into a cab. "I had a nice time."

"I'll call you," he promised in that high, lying voice men use when they're eager to escape a situation.

Allie never saw him at Leopards again.


*Allie spent the* rest of the night and most of the next day refining her concept. That evening she pitched it to Angela backstage at the club.

"Celebrity look-alike call girls."

Angela got the concept immediately, and encouraged by her enthusiasm, Allie organized a meeting at her apartment, inviting the specific women needed to make her idea work. She wore her best business attire and treated the whole event as though she was pitching to a Fortune 500 company.

"I got an idea when I went to see *Legends*," Allie told the meeting.

"I auditioned for that show," interrupted Malfi. "The director said I couldn't sing a lick. The nerve of that prick."

"You can't sing, Malfi," said Angela. "Shut up and let Allie speak."

Malfi sullenly leaned back into the threadbare sofa and listened.

"This is the town of the fake," Allie continued. "The

pretend Eiffel Tower. The pretend Venice. The pretend New York skyline."

Allie opened up that week's copy of *Neon*, the pullout entertainment section of the local paper. "'Tribute to Neil Diamond. Tribute to Elvis,'" she read. "'American Superstars in Concert. Barbra and Frank Together at Last.' Do you know there are over twenty impersonation shows playing in this town every night? People will pay top dollar to see a copy. I mean, they'll even go to Madame Tussauds at the Venetian to see an imitation made out of wax. They don't care if it's real or not."

"You want us to do a look-alike show?" asked a puzzled Ashley, one of the California coeds who had chosen to abandon her degree and stay in Las Vegas. "When I'm blonde, people say I look like Britney Spears, but I sing like a frog."

Malfi glared at Angela, daring her to make a smart remark.

"No, I don't want to get into the entertainment business," Allie hedged. "Not exactly."

Allie could see that the women looked confused. She continued on. "What's the other entertainment Las Vegas offers?" she asked the group. "One we've all profited from at Leopards?"

They were all looking up at her, waiting to hear the answer.

"Sex," Allie announced. "Sex is the other great Vegas attraction. My idea is to marry the two concepts of celebrity impersonation and sex into a business . . . a business of look-alike call girls."

"Isn't that a fan-fucking-tastic idea?" said Angela encouragingly.

Allie looked around the room. Certainly all the women looked intrigued. "How many times have you been compared to Jennifer Lopez, Malfi?" she asked. "Or Angela to Catherine Zeta-Jones? Or Oneisha to Halle Berry? These women are the unattainable goddesses of our day. And you guys are dead ringers."

"I get that Halle Berry thing all the time," said Oneisha. "I wish I had her money."

"Exactly," Allie said, as she stood to distribute identical folders to each woman. "The most often accessed Internet sites are the ones featuring celebrity nudity. You'll find the statistics in a bar graph on page four," she said. "First Impressions will take those unattainable goddesses and make them attainable."

The room was silent as the women studied the business proposals.

"I've never had sex for money," said Ashley. "I'm not sure I could do it."

"Me, either," said Lulu, a bubbly blonde who looked a lot like Cameron Diaz. "How much do you think we could make?"

"Page eight," Allie replied.

The women all hurriedly turned to page eight of their folders. Malfi let out a long whistle as she read the numbers.

"If there's one thing I learned working at Heaven," said Allie, "it was that expensive and exclusive is the way to go in this town. We'll charge five thousand dollars a time. I keep two thousand, you keep three. That's a better deal than anyone else offers in Vegas. Plus, I'll pay all expenses, including rigorous security."

Allie paused to gauge the group's reaction. Nobody spoke. She knew this was the pivotal moment of the meeting. "Hands up if you're in," she asked slowly. "No pressure. If it's not for you, that's cool, too."

The women all looked at each other. Shrugs and nods were exchanged. One by one each raised a hand.

"Ladies, welcome to First Impressions," said Allie triumphantly. *Two hundred grand,* she thought, *here I come.*

# SIXTEEN

Across town, Christian Sacco was getting ready to tour a project he loathed. He had disliked the maternity ward/ funeral home concept from the moment his ex-girlfriend had pitched it. At each stage of its forward development, he was certain that Richard Summerford would suddenly come to his senses and completely cancel the Hello Goodbye project. However, here they were on the eve of the official unveiling of the casino's latest offering and Summerford was still heavily attached to the scheme he had initiated. It was, however, Christian who bore the brunt of responsibility for its failure or success, a fact that pissed him off enormously whenever he thought about it.

The board had made the announcement three months ago that Richard Summerford would be stepping down and would be replaced by Christian Sacco. Acknowledging his lame-duck status, Richard had already moved on to an office in corporate headquarters and Christian had taken over the premier office he had coveted from his first day of employment at Heaven. Unlike Richard, Christian had redecorated. He had chosen a much-lauded interior designer who had garnered great reviews for two futuristic nightclubs she had created in Los Angeles. As a result, Christian's office now looked like a futuristic nightclub. His white ostrich leather chair was trimmed with purple neon piping that lit up each time he sat down, and his glass desk filled with tropical fish needed its water changed at least once a week.

Hello Good-bye's two new buildings were situated at the rear of the hotel, in the empty space between Heaven and Frank Sinatra Drive, the parallel slip road that ran behind all the important casinos located on the west side of the Strip. This road now accessed a separate entrance to the new facilities: Cars containing the pregnant would enter the complex and turn left, and hearses containing the deceased would turn right. Both annexes, of course, fed into the main casino, and it was at this entrance that the main management of Heaven now stood, waiting to conduct a final walk-through of the new additions to the property.

Christian strode through his casino and toward the meeting. Frank DiPaulo trailed by Christian's side, having made an effortless transition from old master to new. Much to Christian's annoyance, Richard Summerford was also there, determined to see the project through its final stage.

"I appreciate you coming today. I know this was an inconvenience," said Christian, meaning that Richard's presence was superfluous.

"I've just come in an advisory capacity. Pretend I'm not here," said Richard, meaning he was still really in charge.

The group of casino executives filed into the passage that led to the maternity wing. Six months into construction, a wag on the building staff had nicknamed this corridor "the birth canal." Richard had overheard the remark and decided to make it a reality. The hallway they were now traveling along was indeed an oversized but anatomically correct replica of a woman's parturient passage.

When rehearsing a new entertainment show, casinos often use their own employees as audience guinea pigs for tryout performances before embarking on the real thing in front of actual paying customers. Christian had decided the same system should be employed in this instance as well, so twelve expectant employees were at this moment in labor within a dozen of the ornate birthing suites that satellited off the main reception area that the walk-through management group now entered.

"Welcome to Creation," breathed Natalie, an immaculately uniformed and beautiful receptionist with a perfect smile and abundant breasts.

Natalie sat in front of a bank of discreetly positioned computer screens that video-linked her to all of the birthing suites.

"Everything going OK?" Christian asked hurriedly, determined to speak before Richard and thereby establish his ultimate on-property authority.

"Yes, Mr. Sacco," reported Natalie. "Mrs. Masini gave birth at nine fifty-two and is resting comfortably. Mrs. Berming is about to deliver, and six of our other mothers are in active labor."

"Everything working well in reception?" interjected Richard. "Any complaints?"

It was hard to see how there could be any complaints regarding the sumptuously outfitted reception area. Modeled in the style of a hip, boutique hotel, the waiting room contained various food stations, a bar, a smoking room, and, of course, gambling. Not only were the usual games and machines on offer, but expectant fathers were also free to gamble on the weight, the sex, the arrival time, and even the eye color of their soon-to-be-arriving child.

"We ran out of sushi five minutes ago," admitted Natalie.

"Crystal," barked Christian, looking around for his senior VP of food and beverage.

Crystal Gates already had her cell phone clamped to her ear. "I'm on it, Christian," she growled through her desiccated lips.

"Let's move on," Richard ordered.

The spotless maternity ward looked more like a TV soap opera hospital set than a working medical facility. Everything, including the doctors and nurses, was pristine and antiseptic, an aura heightened by the classical music piped into the corridors designed to instill a pervasive sense of calm. Several of the birthing rooms were uni-

form in design, but there were also a few uniquely decorated rooms for the more adventurous and imaginative. It
was into one of these rooms, code-named Waterworld,
that the group of executives now ventured.

Three plumbers were working on the large twenty-by-
twenty bath pool that dominated the room while the
newly appointed manager of Creation, Paula McCarthy,
looked on.

"Good morning, everyone," said Paula as all the executives awkwardly attempted to gain access to the water-
birthing room, each determined not to be left out in the
corridor.

"What's our ultimate fix on the drainage situation,
Paula?" asked Paul Hornsucker, senior VP of hotel operations.

"We're confident we have a handle on it," said Paula.
"There was a possible challenge with the speed of
drainage due to the amount of water, so we wanted to go
above and beyond and make sure we met the challenge
proactively."

"How long was it taking to drain?" asked Richard Summerford.

"Twenty-four hours," Paula replied. "But plumbing's
come up with a creative solution and we've got that down
to two."

"That allows us to perform up to three water-births a
day," interrupted Paul Hornsucker. "It's a specialized
service, so we're envisaging demand on that room never
exceeding two per day anyway."

"How does it work?" asked Frank DiPaulo. "What's the
point of it?"

"It lessens the pressure on the cervix," said Brianna Murphy, the new VP of database marketing, who still had nightmares about the ordeal of giving birth to her own son, Mark. "It's supposed to reduce the pain by up to eighty percent."

"Why doesn't the baby drown?" asked Frank.

"Let me page the head doctor on duty," said Paula. "She'll be happy to explain the whole process in detail."

"Not necessary," said Christian abruptly. "Let's move on to the Graceland room."

The Graceland room had been Christian's contribution to the Hello Good-bye project. Elvis was still synonymous with Las Vegas and Christian felt that if there was a demand for an Elvis wedding, why not for an Elvis birth? The search for an obstetrician who was both able and willing to masquerade as Elvis in his later years was not as difficult as initially feared, and indeed it was this doctor, dressed in the trademark sequined jumpsuit, sunglasses, and sideburns, who now greeted them at the entrance to the Graceland birthing room. The only indication of the man's several years of medical training was the solid-gold stethoscope dangling around his neck.

"I hear Mrs. Masini's delivery went well," Christian said as he shook Elvis's hand.

"Than' you very much," said the Elvis doctor.

Christian peered through the replicated gates of Graceland and into the room that was decorated in the style of the King's own master bedroom in Memphis.

"Are they still here?" asked Christian.

"Mother and daughter have left the building," Elvis announced.

"Keep up the good work," Christian told Elvis.

"TCB," Elvis responded with a trademark flicker of his upper lip. "Taking care of birthing."

"I have a three o'clock, Christian," said Richard Summerford, glancing at his watch. "Let's move on to the funeral side."

Richard firmly believed Departures could do to mortuaries what Starbucks had done to coffee bars. Funerals had been generic and uniform for centuries. The baby-boomer generation was going to change all that. Thematic, individualized funerals were the wave of the future.

Twelve funeral stations had been built and an album of backdrops, props, music, and caskets had been assembled so relatives could make a selection that best suited the deceased subject being honored. Themes included a rodeo, Hawaii, the military, golf, space, Elvis (again), ancient civilizations, water, fire, favorite TV programs, and, of course, Vegas itself.

A middle-aged woman from Henderson was selecting a funeral for her late mother when the walk-through executive committee arrived to inspect the facility.

"We're sorry for your loss," said Christian, attempting sympathy by repeating a line he'd heard on a television drama. "Have you encountered any problems? Apart from your mother dying, of course."

"Everyone's been wonderful," Mrs. Beekman attested. "Ma was an avid golfer and the golf package is just perfect. It's Ma all the way. This is exactly what she would have wanted."

"We were just discussing the possibility of a final ceremony on the casino's golf range," explained the head funeral director. "Mrs. Beekman likes the idea of filling golf balls with her mother's ashes and then letting the mourners hit the balls out onto the range."

"We'd play her favorite song while we did it," explained Mrs. Beekman. "'In The Mood,' by Glenn Miller."

"What a perfectly wonderful way to honor your mother," said Richard. "Christian, everything here seems splendid. I have complete confidence in everyone. I'll be in touch."

Before Christian could respond, Richard Summerford had turned and left.

"You could put her photo on them," said Frank DiPaulo.

"What?" said Christian irritably.

"On the golf balls. Put her mother's photo on them."

Mrs. Beekman's face lit up at the thought.

"Action that, please," ordered Christian. "At the casino's cost."

And with that beneficent gesture Christian turned and led his troops away from what was to prove to be one of Heaven's most profitable projects in recent history.


"*Dazzle me, people,*" Christian ordered at the following Monday-morning executive meeting. The success of the Hello Good-bye project was wearing on Christian. He wanted his own success. "I want out-of-the-box ideas."

"I had an idea," Brianna Murphy said softly. Brianna had been waiting for an opportunity like this since joining the company six months earlier after a decade working for a prestigious Wall Street investment bank.

"Shoot," ordered Christian.

"I've been studying the poker phenomenon," Brianna

continued. "In 1982 the World Series of Poker attracted fifty-two entries. Last year it attracted over five thousand."

"Are you suggesting we expand the poker room, Brianna?" Christian asked impatiently.

"I'm suggesting we locate and help create the next phenomenon," Brianna replied. "If someone had been able to predict the rise in popularity of poker ten years ago, and been able to monopolize the TV rights, that person would now control a billion-dollar industry."

A billion dollars. Now we're talking. Christian leaned forward in his chair. "Go on," he said.

"Two inventions accounted for poker's ascendancy," said Brianna, as she began to open the file she had now removed from her briefcase and placed on the table. "The Internet, which allowed people to play online, and the miniaturized camera, which allowed TV audiences to see hole cards."

Christian noticed everybody but one person at the meeting was hanging on Brianna's every word. Jimmy Falanucci was doodling on his Heaven notepad, clearly disinterested in what Brianna, or anyone else, had to say. Christian had noticed Jimmy's recent apathy and made a mental note to talk to his head of security about the problem. Perhaps Jimmy was burned out and needed replacing. He had a bored listlessness about him that Christian found irritating. Maybe he was on a diet and that was making him grumpy. He'd certainly lost weight. Meanwhile, Brianna was spreading graphs and sheets on the conference table.

"Poker has been a popular game for centuries. In America, it became a saloon hit when the country was being settled. My research team went back to see if there were any other games that had enjoyed similar or greater popularity."

"And . . . ?" asked Christian.

"There was one," said Brianna, unable to mask a sly grin of triumph and excitement. "One game has been played in every civilized culture and by every generation for centuries. It's a game that I believe is ripe for modernization and exploitation."

Brianna looked around the table at the raised eyebrows and expectant expressions.

"Dominoes," she announced.

"Explain," said Christian.

"What I'm suggesting," continued Brianna, "is that we create and host the World Series of Dominoes. We bring a cable channel in for TV exposure. We bring in a high-profile host. We create a sexy buzz around dominoes. That's what happened with poker; that's what we can do with dominoes."

"How do you create a sexy buzz around dominoes?" asked Christian.

"How do you create a sexy buzz around anything?" replied Brianna. "You make the props look cool . . . make the tiles glow or something. You get great-looking women to stand around in their underwear. You invite Hollywood and rock-and-roll types to join in the action. You give the whole thing gangsta 'tude. Make it happening. What's so sexy about poker? Five years ago it was a bunch of fat old guys smoking cigars. Now it's cool. Go figure."

Christian hated the idea and that excited him. He'd hated the Hello Good-bye idea and look how successful that had been. He'd hated the snake restaurant and it had become the hottest eatery in town.

"Run with it, Brianna. See if the figures stack up," Christian ordered.

Christian got up and all the other executives followed his example. "Jimmy, can I see you in my office for a moment?" Christian asked Falanucci.

Jimmy Falanucci followed Christian into his office, sat down at the glass desk, and stared at the tropical fish swimming in its legs.

"Everything OK?" Christian asked.

Everything was not OK with Jimmy Falanucci, but the last person he wanted to share that with was Christian Sacco. "I'm fine," he lied. "A bit run down."

"Then take a fucking pill," Christian ordered. "You're setting a bad example to the younger members of staff."

Jimmy stood up. "Is that all?" he asked tersely.

"For now," said Christian.

"Good."

Jimmy started to leave. At the door, he turned and gestured toward Christian's desk. "One of your fish is dead," he told him.

Christian sighed and picked up the phone. He had the pet store on speed dial. "This is Christian Sacco. I need to have my desk drained again."

# SEVENTEEN

Like many people, Allie had always assumed prostitution was somehow legal in Las Vegas, and was surprised to find out it wasn't, given its strong advertising presence in the town. Allie wondered how so much of her local yellow pages could be dedicated to advertisements for "Full Service Buxom Blondes" and "Asian Centerfolds Direct to You." She suspected it had something to do with the ads being filed under "E" for "entertainment" rather than "H" for "hooker." A few discreet inquiries confirmed Allie's hunch. It all had to do with the Supreme Court having upheld outcall dancing (girls coming to your hotel room to "dance") as an art form. This was the loophole that allowed billboards to sell "Barely Legal Party Girls" to passing motorists and would allow Allie to launch First Impressions.

Allie had always had a flair for design. With the help of a local print shop, she concocted a killer graphic that featured Angela as Catherine Zeta-Jones, Ashley as Britney Spears, and Malfi as J-Lo. The slug line positioned above the phone number—"Would You Like to Swing on a Star?"—was the perfect tease.

Allie decided to go with a new form of advertising she'd recently admired: mobile billboards. A truck pulling a ten-by-twenty-foot image moved slowly around to specific spots, allowing the advertiser to better target its audience. Allie used what remained of her savings to rent two trucks for a month to carry her message to the Strip, the convention centers, the airport, lunchtime restaurants, and, late at night, the strip clubs.

Meanwhile, Allie's girls were doing their part and refining their impersonations. Much time was spent in spas and hair salons, poring over photos in magazines so that the fantasies could be visually fully realized. Allie also had the women study videotapes of each particular target, so that a vocal impression and particular signature mannerisms could be attempted as well. Allie had learned stripping and hooking were largely all about acting, so she was not surprised at how accomplished at mimicry the girls quickly became. Now they just needed the johns.

First Impressions' target market was a classy, affluent man with major discretionary income. This type of man tended to stay on the Strip. Allie had visited all the concierges, bellmen, valet parkers, and casino hosts that she knew and explained her business concept. She had even offered to pay five hundred dollars for each introduction.

Allie had Sprint install two new phone lines in her apartment. Both lines started ringing the first morning the advertising trucks lumbered onto the roads. Allie had expected the callers to be slightly embarrassed and sheepish. Instead, most were demanding and incredibly specific.

"I want Britney for an hour. But I want the Britney in the 'Oops! . . . I Did It Again' video. Schoolgirl outfit. Pigtails. I don't want fat Britney."

Allie was kept so busy she had to employ her next-door neighbor, Maggie Fein, to help answer the phones. Maggie had an attractive voice that some callers found intriguing.

"What do you look like, baby?" a man's voice would ask.

"Me?" said Maggie, using her most sultry tone. "I'm twenty-two, five-foot-three, and I weigh a hundred pounds. I've got blue eyes, big boobs, long legs. I'm only wearing a thong, and you'll never guess what I have in my mouth right now."

This always made Allie laugh. Sixty-year-old Maggie weighed over 250, invariably wore a sweat suit to cover her shapeless body, and usually had a candy bar in her mouth.

Right from the start, First Impressions was a bigger hit than Allie had even dared hoped for. Soon she was adding Heather Graham, Kate Hudson, Lucy Liu, Jennifer Aniston, and Serena and Venus Williams to her roster. She regretfully had to turn down a Hillary Clinton doppelgänger on the basis that the demand would be slight.

The only negative was the lack of business coming from all the hotel contacts Allie had primed. That surprised her. She wondered if somehow Christian had poisoned that avenue for her. Her suspicion was strengthened one morning when her doorbell was rung by her old coworker Jimmy Falanucci. Was he here to warn her off? She opened the door and gave him her best attempt at a welcoming smile.

"Jimmy! What a great surprise! How are you?" she gushed.

Allie didn't need an answer to "How are you?" It was clear Jimmy was sick. He had lost maybe thirty pounds and was the color of oatmeal.

"Hi, Allie. Good to see ya. Can I come in?"

Jimmy hobbled in and collapsed onto Allie's sofa.

"This isn't gonna be easy, Allie. I've got something to tell you that you ain't gonna like."

So she was right. Maybe he was going to warn her to keep her girls out of Heaven.

Jimmy pulled two compact discs out of the left pocket of the jeans jacket that hung baggily on his gaunt figure.

"About ten years ago I was working in Atlantic City. So was Christian Sacco. So was my daughter," Jimmy said. "Can I smoke?"

"Sure. Let me get you an ashtray."

Allie went into the kitchenette and found Jimmy a saucer. When she returned, he had his eyes closed.

"Jimmy," she said softly.

His eyelids opened slowly. He pulled out a packet of cigarettes and lit one. "A young hoodlum dated my daughter. First date, he raped her. I went crazy and beat the guy up. I beat him up bad."

"I see," said Allie, not quite sure why she was being told this story.

"I killed him, Allie," said Jimmy. "He had a weak heart. I didn't know. I killed him."

Allie said nothing.

"Christian Sacco knew a guy who knew a guy high up in the Philly police. Turned out this guy had a daughter the same age as mine, so he was sympathetic. The punk kid was a nothing. In the country illegally. Nobody gave a rat's ass about him. Christian got it all covered up. Made it go away. As a favor to me."

"Quite a favor."

"Tell me about it. I owed him big-time and he never let me forget it. That's why I had to do to you what he asked me to do."

Allie felt her heartbeat quicken.

"I think I know why he wanted you gone," continued Jimmy. "That singer in the lounge was someone's girl-friend. Christian was getting brown-bagged to keep her in there even though she sounded like a walrus with lar-yngitis."

Jimmy began to cough a terrible hacking cough that seemed to start from somewhere near his toes.

Allie got up and fetched her guest a glass of water. It all made sense now. She had been so stupid. How many times had she wondered how Christian afforded the clothes he bought and the lifestyle he enjoyed? Of course he was on the take. She had dug her own grave by insist-ing that Malfi be replaced.

"The boyfriend was the counterfeiter, not your patsy magician. He and Christian ripped a coupla hundred grand out of the joint before the chip design could be altered," explained Jimmy. "Watch these discs. It's all on there, including a meeting I had with Christian when he asked me to deliver the counterfeiting equipment to your ex-husband's workshop. The cap I wore had a concealed video camera. You'll see how he planned it."

"Why are you telling me this now?" Allie asked, suspecting the answer.

"I'm dying, Allie," Jimmy said. "Lung cancer. I've only got a few more months. There's nothing Christian Sacco can do to me now."

"I'm sorry to hear that, Jimmy," she said.

"Yeh, well, shouldn't have smoked five million cigarettes, I guess," said Jimmy ruefully. "I'm going back East to spend time with my daughter and her husband. Please accept my apology, Allie. Christian Sacco's a dangerous scumbag. If you use these discs to go after him, you be careful how you do it. If he finds out you've got them, he'll come after you."

His quivering hand offered up the discs and Allie took them.

"Want my advice? It might be better to just go on with your life. I hear you've got a new business you just started up."

So Jimmy did know about First Impressions.

"Your kickback's too low, by the way," Jimmy told her.

"What? It's twice everyone else's. They're only offering two fifty. I'm offering five hundred bucks an introduction," Allie protested.

Jimmy smiled. "When your competitors heard your idea, they raised their kickback to seven fifty. Guess you got 'em scared. Bye, Allie. You take care."

"You, too."

Allie watched the DVDs as soon as Jimmy left. It was all there, including the piece of surveillance tape Christian had made Jimmy edit out of their lunch meeting in

Pandora's Lunchbox. At first, Allie felt awful as she relived the injustice both she and Barry had suffered. Then the more she thought about it, the better she felt. She had something that could bring Christian down. The tide had turned and the power had shifted. The only question now was how far she could make Christian fall. Timing was everything. Sure, she could take the discs to the authorities now and get Christian in trouble and Barry out of it. But Barry was nearing the end of his sentence and, paperwork being what it was, it probably wouldn't make that much difference to how long he stayed in jail. Allie wanted the most public humiliation possible for Christian. If she had to wait for the perfect circumstance to exact revenge, then she would wait. Waiting wasn't a problem.

Allie made the kickback adjustment Jimmy had suggested, and business doubled. First Impressions was on fire. Money was rolling in. Allie's biggest problem was keeping up with demand. She added two more phone lines, another operator (a friend of Maggie's who was wheelchair bound) and ten more girls; she now had two Britneys, three Beyoncés, and a Pamela Anderson who could also do Jessica Simpson.

Late one afternoon, an exhausted Allie was looking forward to taking a well-deserved, relaxing, strawberry-scented bubble bath after a strenuous four days of phone calls and bookings. This had been First Impressions most successful long weekend yet, and she had booked almost a hundred thousand dollars' worth of business.

Bruno, the bouncer from Leopards, was now on Allie's payroll as well. He had just phoned in to report that

Malfi's assignment had been completed and she was safely in her brand-new Lexus convertible and on her way home. Bruno himself was now driving to the other end of the Strip to make sure that all went well with Oneisha's date. Oneisha's client had requested to reenact the sex scene between Halle Berry and Billy Bob Thornton from the movie *Monster's Ball.* It was the fifth time Oneisha had been asked to re-create this particular tableau in as many weeks. Men who bought sex had very little imagination, Allie decided.

She was just about to add thirty seconds of cold water so as to render the bath the perfect Allie temperature when her emergency hotline rang. This was a phone she'd had installed for the exclusive use of the girls and she scampered to answer it.

"Houston, we have a problem."

It was Angela. "What's wrong?" Allie asked hurriedly.

"You know I have that regular football thing, right?"

"Of course."

Allie had twice previously booked Angela and Ashley to play Catherine Zeta-Jones and Renée Zellweger as cheerleaders while a certain septuagenarian high roller called Marvin watched the Green Bay Packers while wearing just his underwear and socks. Ashley's usual impersonation was Britney Spears, but Marvin loved the film *Chicago* about as much as he did Brett Favre, and Ashley found adding a squint to Britney acceptably transformed her into Renée.

"Ashley's bailed on me. She's a no-show."

Allie was later to find out that Ashley's mother and father had paid their daughter an unexpected visit. Ashley was at the exact moment of Angela's call trapped in a Ford Explorer, being forcibly driven back to Los Angeles by two pissed-off parents who, through the employment of a private investigator, had found out what their daughter really did for a living.

"*Monday Night Football* starts in less than an hour, Allie," said Angela. "What do you want me to do? If I lose this money, I'm not gonna be happy."

Allie flipped through a mental Rolodex of available girls. All were booked except Malfi, who could never pass as Renée Zellweger. "Can you do a single and jump around twice as much?" Allie asked.

"It's not gonna fly, girl. He's uncomplicated, but fussy. He booked two. He wants two."

Allie knew that Marvin had never touched the girls. He just enjoyed watching them dance between the commercials and at halftime.

"Allie . . . ," whispered Angela. "It's easy. You can be here in thirty minutes. The game starts at six."

"What do you mean?" said Allie quickly.

"You know what I mean," Angela replied. "You look more like Renée Zellweger than Ashley does. You twirl a pom-pom around for some shaky old guy. Big deal."

Allie's mouth felt suddenly dry. She *had* been a cheerleader at school.

"It's time to step up and take one for the team, girlfriend," urged Angela. "Face it. This is the business you're in. Time to get a little dirty."

"I just don't think I could," said Allie.

"Oh, enough of that bullshit," snapped Angela. "You'll send us all out there to do God knows what, but you're too precious to do a little dance? What sort of sisterhood is that?"

"I know, I know," moaned Allie, knowing she was being manipulated, but still feeling that Angela's argument had some merit.

"You're supposed to be the fixer," said Angela calmly into the phone. "That's why we pay you. So fix it."

Allie took a deep breath. "I'll meet you in front of reception at Caesars in twenty minutes," she announced.

Angela was pleased.

"Great," she said. "Except this trip he's not at Caesars. This time he's staying at Heaven."

Allie had not returned to Heaven since the day Richard Summerford had ordered her forcible ejection. Even though she was heavily disguised, wearing a blonde wig and sunglasses, she was nervous of bumping into anyone she knew. She hurried from the public parking lot and into reception, panicking when she could not locate Angela anywhere among the crowd of hotel customers and luggage.

"Allie! Allie! Over here!"

Allie spun around and saw Angela waving wildly from Cosmos. Cosmos had been one of the first innovations Richard Summerford had introduced after the hotel had opened. He had thought of the idea while watching a rerun of *Star Wars* on TV. The concept of a futuristic bar was not in itself novel, but the fully automated, perfectly anatomical topless robotic waitresses Richard had commissioned Sony to build made Cosmos unique.

Allie plonked herself down opposite Angela.

"Drink?" Angela asked.

"Do we have time?"

Angela glanced at her watch. "Ten minutes to kickoff. We're OK. Drew isn't even here yet."

Allie ordered a vodka martini, straight up with extra olives. She had a feeling she would be requiring the fortification.

"This is the easiest gig in the world," explained Angela. "Leave all the talking to me. When we get in the room, we'll go to the bathroom and get changed. We do our thing during every commercial break. We hang out with Marvin at halftime and chitchat about the game. We split at the end of the game or if he falls asleep. Easy McPeasy. Here's Drew."

Drew was another of Allie's security detail. An ex-football player with a blown-out knee and a broken NFL dream, Drew cut an imposing figure as he walked across reception to meet them.

"Watch the game in the sports book, Drew," ordered Allie. "If we're not back within five minutes after the game ends, come find us in . . ."

Allie looked inquiringly at Angela.

"Suite 9542," she supplied.

Angela picked up the Louis Vuitton tote bag containing her and Ashley's various Marvin props and stood up. "Ready?"

Allie gulped down the rest of her martini and got up as well. "No. But let's do this anyway."

Five minutes later, they were outside the door to the suite.

"Remember. Let me do the talking," warned Angela as she knocked on the door.

For two minutes there was no answer.

"Maybe he's dead," hoped Allie.

Just then the door opened to reveal a wizened old man wearing a Heaven bathrobe, a hearing aid, and black socks. "I was just going to come looking for you," he said. "Why didn't you knock?"

"Hiya, handsome," said Angela and pushed Allie inside.

"Who's this?" Marvin asked Angela, pointing at Allie.

His penis and his hearing might have softened, but his eyesight was as sharp as ever.

"Marvin, you're in luck. Ashley had a family emergency and Shannon, the top girl in our agency, was available."

Marvin scrutinized Allie as closely as he would an application for a jumbo mortgage. "She's good. She's a little more Gwyneth than Renée, but she'll be a nice change."

"Hi," said Allie meekly.

"Shannon, tell me, do you have any cheerleading experience?"

"Captain."

"Ashley can do split jumps. Can you?"

"My skill was cartwheels."

"That sounds good to me. The game's about to start. It's a good one. Packers against the Giants."

"We'll go get ready," said Angela breathily.

Allie followed Angela into the bathroom. "This is too weird."

"It's one of the easier gigs," Angela replied, beginning to remove her clothes and fold them in a neat pile on the dressing table. She then opened her bag and handed Allie two oversized yellow pom-poms.

"Where's my cheerleading outfit?" asked Allie.

"That's it," Angela replied, gesturing toward the pom-poms.

"I don't understand."

"We're naked. What aren't you understanding?"

"I'm jumping up and down naked?" Allie screeched.

"No. I'm jumping up and down naked," Angela began to laugh. "You're doing cartwheels, remember?"

Allie began to slip off her skirt. "I'm keeping my bra and panties on. I don't care what you say."

"It's not what *I* say. We're here to please Marvin."

Allie reluctantly removed her underwear, grabbed her two pom-poms, and steeled herself for humiliation. Angela opened the bathroom door and out they bounced.

Two twentysomething men now sat in the suite with Marvin.

"Hi, girls," said one. "What's shaking? Apart from your titties that is."

The other man high-fived his friend.

"Good one, Talan. He shoots, he scores."

Allie froze in horror.

"Did I tell you my nephews joined me on this trip?" asked Marvin.

"No, you didn't," said Allie, backing up toward the bathroom door.

"It's gonna cost more," Angela told Marvin.

"Not a problem," said Marvin, peeling hundred-dollar bills from the stack he had in his robe pocket.

Angela shrugged. "Fine with me."

"Not fine with me," said Allie. "This is not going to happen."

The guy called Talan got up quickly and stood between Allie and the bathroom door. "Now is that any way to treat our uncle?" he said. "After he's been such a good customer."

"I'm not a hooker," said Allie.

Talan laughed. "Yeh, right. Kevin, do you believe this crap, man?"

"Hey, if my friend says it's no, then it's no," said Angela.

"Bullshit," said Talan, laughing. He was a big guy and picked up naked 110-pound Allie with ease, carrying her into one of the suite's bedrooms.

"No rough stuff, boys," said Marvin, looking concerned and ineffectual.

"We're just having some fun, Uncle," said Kevin as he grabbed Angela by the arm and pushed her toward another bedroom. "Relax. They're just hookers."

Talan pushed Allie through the bedroom door, closed it with his foot, and threw her onto the bed.

"I have a bodyguard downstairs," said Allie. "If you touch me, he'll hurt you. He'll hurt you bad."

"Am I missing something here?" said Talan as he removed his pants. "Isn't this the business you're in? I'm not a horrible-looking guy. What's your problem?"

As he advanced toward her, a terrified Allie looked around for a weapon. The lamp on the side of the bed looked heavy, but it wasn't within her reach.

Allie heard a commotion next door. Evidently, Angela was in as much trouble as she was.

"You have to believe me. This isn't what I normally do," begged Allie.

"Oh, please," said Talan dismissively. "You dance around naked for some old guy. How disgusting is that?"

As he placed one knee on the bed and readied to pounce on Allie, the bedroom door flew open. Talan looked around and saw his friend Kevin staggering through the door, clutching his testicles.

"Bitch kneed me in the balls."

Allie sensed an opportunity. She grabbed the lamp from the bedside table and struck Talan on the back of the head.

"Owww!"

He fell off the bed and onto his knees.

"Come on, Allie," Angela screamed from the living room. "Let's go."

Allie ran past both men and through the door to the corridor, which Angela was holding open. "My clothes," gasped Allie.

"I've got them," said Angela. "Let's go."

They dressed in the elevator and left the hotel before Security could catch them. Drew drove both of them home and Allie cried uncontrollably all the way there.

"C'mon, Allie, what kinda business did you think we were in?" asked Angela gently. "Shit happens. The good news is it doesn't happen very often."

Allie knew it would never happen to her again. They'd had a close call. Very close. Barry was getting out in two weeks and she had over a quarter of a million dollars in the bank. First Impressions had done its job. It was now time to walk away from it and toward the future.

# EIGHTEEN

Allie found herself preparing for Barry's release as though preparing for a date. Two days before the event, she visited her favorite hair salon to get her highlights refreshed and her fingers and toes manicured. She splurged on a sexy new outfit she found on sale at her favorite boutique—a red, microfiber halter-top with a black front-slit skirt—and spent more care than usual applying her makeup. Anxious not to be late, she drove out to the prison compound an hour before the appointed time of Barry's release and leaned nervously against her car, willing Barry to walk through the checkpoint guardhouse. Thirty minutes later than scheduled, she finally spotted him and began waving frantically. Barry saw her and stopped dead. He leaned against the side of the guardhouse as though emotionally overcome, raised his hands to his head, and took an imaginary photograph of her with an imaginary camera. Then he sauntered over to her.

"You aaiigght?" he asked.

"Am I what?" she said, pulling him into her bosom and hugging him tightly.

This Barry was a different human being to the one who had been incarcerated fifteen months ago; not only mentally different, but physically, too. The daily weight-pile workouts had really changed his physiognomy.

"You need a new suit," said Allie, appraising him. "This one's about three sizes too small."

"Never mind a new suit," said Barry, enjoying breathing in Allie's perfume. "I need a new life."

They talked very little on the drive back to Las Vegas. Allie was anxious to give Barry space to decompress. She was also anxious not to say the wrong thing. God knows what he'd had to experience in there. The last thing she wanted to do was make him relive it by talking about it. However, to talk about anything else would just seem crass. So instead she smiled encouragingly, occasionally reaching across the seat to give his thigh a welcoming squeeze. When the moment felt right, she said, "Look in the glove compartment."

Barry did. There was an envelope inside with his name on it.

"Open it," said Allie. "It's not two hundred thousand, Barry, but I did my best."

"Allie, anything will help," said Barry, opening the envelope. "Of course I didn't expect you to raise two hundred grand. That was just crazy talk. I just need enough to start small in a lounge somewhere. Then I can build up a bankroll, afford to build the tricks one by one, and within a few years I might . . ."

Barry looked at the check in his hand and gasped.

"But . . . how . . . I mean . . . you're kidding, right?" he spluttered.

Allie laughed, enjoying Barry's flabbergasted expression. "The check's good, Barry," she said. "I'll explain to you much later how I did it; but believe me, the check's good."

Barry kissed the check. He kissed Allie. He kissed the check again.

"I can't believe this," he said. "This is too weird. Thank you, Allie. I won't let you down, I promise. I owe you. I really owe you."

Allie shook her head. "You'll never owe me, Barry," she said with feeling. "I'll always owe you. Always."

Back in the city, she took him to her apartment, where his first request was to take a shower that might possibly last three weeks. While he washed up, Allie drove to the mall to buy him some larger, casual clothes. When she returned, she found a naked, comatose Barry fast asleep in her bed. She hung his new clothes up in her wardrobe. He didn't stir. She slipped gently into the chair beside the wardrobe and stared at him. Her comforter had slipped down the bed and Barry's chest was exposed. There was no denying it, he looked very hot. She slipped her shoes off and considered her options. She was kind of tired herself after that long, dusty drive. She removed her skirt. It wasn't like they hadn't done it lots of times before, she rationalized, pulling her top over her head. It would be like a really personal welcome-home present. She unhooked her bra and dropped it to the floor. Pulling down her panties, she slipped into the bed. Barry woke up.

"Klepto, what the fuck are you doing?" Barry asked. "Oh. Allie, it's you."

Allie was mortified. "I'm sorry, Barry. I thought you'd like it," she said, trying to clamber out of the bed.

"I do. I do. Come here, silly," said Barry, grabbing her and pulling her back in.

They kissed. And they kissed. And they kissed. Lots of kissing. Anything more than kissing, though, proved problematic.

"It's like trying to push a marshmallow into a piggy bank," moaned Barry. "I've never had this problem before."

"After all you've been through," said Allie diplomatically, "it's completely understandable. Don't worry. We'll try again later. Let's just cuddle."

They tried again later. Marshmallow. Piggy bank.

Barry felt annoyed and humiliated. The first two times it happened (or rather didn't happen), Barry rationalized that it was the pressure of the anticipation that was causing his dysfunction. The third time he considered it might just be a sign—a very limp sign.

Allie, on the other hand, was blaming herself. Something had occurred in jail that Barry could not cope with, and if it hadn't been for her relationship with Christian, Barry would never have gone to prison in the first place. It was all her fault. Again.

Defeated, the couple got dressed and went for a drink at the Aviary, a bar that had opened near Allie's apartment.

Three of the six parakeets in the cage behind the bar appeared to squawk in Barry's direction.

"This might be me projecting, but I think they recognize you," Allie said.

"They did spend a lot of time in my pants. I guess you

don't forget a thing like that," agreed Barry, grabbing their drinks.

"I made sure the Jackson Three were well taken care of while you were away," Allie assured him, moving toward a free table. "If you want them back, the manager said it wouldn't be a problem."

Barry smiled and shook his head. "I don't think they want to be associated with a jailbird."

Allie half-laughed and then yet another awkward silence descended between them. Barry decided to broach the subject that was on both their minds.

"Let's talk some more about my pants," he ventured.

"It's just a phase," Allie replied quickly.

"It's not a phase, Allie. I have to tell you something."

Allie concentrated very hard on the glass containing her drink. "It's something that happened in prison, isn't it? What did they do to you?"

"Things happened, but not those kinds of things. My man Klepto kept me safe."

Allie looked up in horror. "'Your man Klepto'?"

Allie had heard of situations like this on cable TV. Had Barry been someone's bitch?

"He wasn't my man . . . he was . . . he'd been to prison a few times before and he . . . let's just call him my guidance counselor."

"I see," Allie replied, not wanting to delve deeper. "Well, I think we just have to give us some more time. We've both been through complete hell."

Barry took Allie's hands in his. "My body's trying to tell me something. It's not meant to be. We're not meant to be."

Allie's eyes filled with tears. It had taken her years to

realize that Barry was the one she really wanted and now he was rejecting her. "It takes two to know when something's not meant to be," she insisted. "And I don't know it and I refuse to believe it."

"I'm not saying it's never meant to be," Barry conceded. "It's just not meant to be at this time. Let's just cool it for a while."

Allie saw the sense in this. They were putting too much pressure on each other. "You're right. We'll just get to know each other slowly again. It was my fault for rushing you into it. Let's just concentrate on your career. I've got so many plans for you."

The old Barry would have said, "Dude, I've just gotten out of prison. Can't I just chill for a while?"

The new Barry said, "Let's talk about that then."

Allie had always believed that Barry's innate charm and bona fide sleight-of-hand skills could be the basis for a killer magic act. She was excited at his new enthusiasm and was anxious to hear all about his ideas. Barry took a gulp of beer, and explained that he had devised a new show-business identity while in prison. Allie was pleased to see the end of "Barry Houdini," but hoped Barry wasn't again going to suggest "Warren Peace," the faux Russian magician.

"Say if you think this is lame, and I'll think of something else," Barry said, shuffling in his seat.

"OK," agreed Allie.

"What if I wear a mask? What if I call myself the Mask? And we let people guess who I am?"

Allie pondered. "I like it. It's a marketing hook. I could do a lot with that."

Encouraged, Barry continued. "I designed so many cool tricks in prison. Different variations on things I found in the warden's books and wild, new ideas I thought up lying awake on my bunk at night. All I needed was the money to make them. And you came through for me, Allie."

"I have another surprise," she revealed. "Do you still have your passport?"

Allie had persuaded Barry to honeymoon in Puerto Vallarta, and he had ordered a passport that he had never used again. An intrigued Barry now leaned forward in his seat. "My passport? Sure. Tell me more."

A couple of months ago, Allie had hit on the idea of initially trying out Barry's show in Australia. There were two great advantages to this plan. First, the American dollar was worth almost two Australian dollars, which meant their money could buy more and stretch further. Second, ten thousand miles away from Nevada, both Allie and Barry could enjoy complete anonymity.

Allie had pitched Barry to all of Australia's casinos and theaters from Darwin to Hobart. She had invested in an impressive presentation package that made Barry look as big a Las Vegas magic hit as David Copperfield or Lance Burton. The Gold Coast Casino, located just behind the vacation playground of Surfer's Paradise in Queensland, nibbled and then bit. Its eleven-hundred-seat theater had lain empty for some months after the demise of its ill-conceived musical revue *G'Day!* Billed as a salute to all things Australian, it had achieved the dubious distinction of appealing to neither tourists nor locals, although the musical staging of the battle of Gallipoli had been hailed as containing all the hallmarks of a camp classic. The deal

Allie offered, by which the casino would receive a third of the gross for no up-front investment, appealed hugely to a casino president who was still smarting from the seven-figure loss sustained by *G'Day!*

"Australia. Wow!" said Barry. "Would I have to do my act upside down?"

"Silly," said Allie, realizing how much she'd missed Barry making her laugh.

"Will I have to put kangaroos down my pants?"

"Of course."

Barry took Allie's hand in his and looked into her eyes.

"Seriously, Allie, I'll do whatever you suggest. I should have listened to you years ago. If you think we should go to Australia, let's go to Australia."

"OK," said Allie, elated at his trust in her and guilty that she had yet to tell him that the trip to Australia was all part of her master plan to take down Christian. Never mind. She would reveal everything when she felt they both were ready.

During the coming weeks, the couple's relationship revolved entirely around business. Allie finalized the Australian deal and Barry refined the drawings and plans for the tricks he had concocted in his jail cell. The Gold Coast Casino had already contractually offered a workshop space with staff and a two-month rehearsal period was planned, during which Barry could both build and perfect his new repertoire.

Allie sold her car and let the lease expire on her apartment. Early one summer morning, the couple traveled by taxi to McCarran Airport and boarded a Qantas flight headed to Brisbane and the new life Barry had requested.

# NINETEEN

"The Indian rope trick was a hoax played by the *Chicago Tribune* over a hundred years ago," Allie announced confidently to the reporters and TV crews staring at her.

She took a sip of water and continued on with her speech. "The eyewitness reports claiming to have seen the trick performed were lies designed to boost the paper's circulation. The *Tribune* admitted the fabrication three months later, but the alleged trick had already seeped into the public's consciousness as a believed urban legend. Many experts have spent years researching the Indian rope trick and all have concluded it's as believable as the Tooth Fairy or Santa Claus."

Allie paused to lend further weight and solemnity to the pronouncement she was about to make. "Today, that conclusion changes forever. Ladies and gentlemen, please welcome the world's greatest magician. The Mask."

Her introduction over, Allie now retreated to one side of the stage and descended into the auditorium to join the members of the Australian media that had responded to the press conference invitation. She had been pleased with

her press release: special black cotton masks manufactured with the invitation embroidered on the back. People
had seemed to like them. Some of the personalities on the
local radio stations had already made comments about
the masks and talked on air about the impending arrival
of the mysterious magician from America.

Today was a slow news day on the Gold Coast of Australia. Nobody had been bitten by a shark; no local politi-
cian had been discovered bedding a hooker; nobody had
eaten bad fish. The press conference therefore was quite
well attended. All the local TV stations and newspapers
had shown up, as well as a stringer for the *Australian,* the
country's only national daily newspaper. Allie was content. She had done her part. Now it was up to Barry. She
offered up a silent prayer that he not revert to his old,
incompetent ways.

Rock music reverberated through the auditorium's
state-of-the-art sound system. The empty stage suddenly
filled with smoke, light, and then Barry, dressed only in a
pair of tight jeans and his signature concealing mask.

Barry had carefully maintained his exercise regimen in
his months since leaving prison, and his exposed, sun-
tanned torso was noticeably cut and muscular. Holding a
lidded basket, Barry moved quickly forward to the front
of the stage and placed the container in plain view,
silently removing the lid. Barry pulled the end of a rope
out of the basket and threw the rope up into the sky.
Apparently defying gravity, the end of the rope somehow
hovered in midair.

"It's done with magnets, mate," Allie heard one journalist whisper to another. "There's a giant magnet up in the roof attracting the end of the rope."

Allie allowed herself a smile. The trick was simpler than that.

Barry now beckoned to a female assistant who joined him from the back of the stage and seemingly began to climb up the rope. As she neared the top of her climb, she quite simply vanished into the ether. First her hands, then her arms, head, torso, and legs disappeared into thin air. This effect produced a genuine gasp from the reporters that was repeated as Barry himself climbed the rope and slowly vanished in front of the watching eyes as well.

The reporter from Channel Seven turned to Allie. "That's impressive," he said with genuine admiration.

"It's not over yet," warned Allie.

The woman's arm fell from the ceiling and onto the stage. A bloody hand followed. Then a head. Two legs. A trunk. Another arm.

Barry's feet next appeared at the top of the rope, followed by the rest of him as he slid down the rope and back onto the stage. Barry collected all the dismembered body parts into a pile and threw a cloth over the scattered remains. As he removed the cloth, the young lady reappeared with all her parts miraculously returned to the right place.

The media applauded enthusiastically.

"How the hell did he do that?" asked one reporter as the curtains closed on Barry and his attractive assistant, still shrouded in the smoky mist.

"Magic," boomed a voice from the rear of the auditorium.

The journalists spun around to see who had spoken. Barry, still masked, was now sitting thirty rows behind them, only a second after the curtain had closed on him a good two hundred feet away.

Barry had used one of the warden's books to find out about Jean-Eugène Robert-Houdin, the acknowledged father of modern magic whom Harry Houdini had taken his name from. Originally a watchmaker, during the early nineteenth century, Robert-Houdin had created intricate tricks from the state-of-the-art clockwork technology available to him at the time. It was this attention to technical detail that had given Barry the idea for the Indian rope trick hologram. Allie had found a company in Sydney that could record a moving holographic image that would project against smoke. Together with Donna, the magician's assistant they had recently hired on the Gold Coast, they had flown to Sydney and recorded the piece that had just wowed the Aussie press. Simple, really, like all good magic.

The members of the press moved toward Barry and started firing questions at him. Barry's good humor and infectious personality played well with them. The casino's experienced head of public relations pulled Allie to one side and assured her that the media coverage would be good. The reporters were impressed by the Mask's talent, but more important, they liked him.

"Do you want to go out to celebrate?" Barry asked Allie after the last few stragglers left the press conference.

"I can't," she said. "I've got to go over the advertising planner with the marketing department."

"I'll come celebrate," said Donna, perkily.

*Oh great,* thought Allie. *He'll probably be able to sleep with her, no problem.*

Allie had hoped that time and a change of country might have inspired a romantic reconnection between her and Barry. It hadn't. As well as everything was going as a business partnership, their personal partnership was a nonstarter.

*Allie's suspicion was* wrong. Barry didn't sleep with Donna after they went for a celebratory drink. He slept with her after his triumphant opening night.

The first show could not have gone better. Barry had built four large tricks as show anchors and then stuffed the rest of the evening with amusing but inconsequential filler tricks. Everything worked. Barry's mask lent the performance a macabre and gothic aura that his boyish charm then undercut with a sly, tongue-in-cheek quality that the audience found both endearing and captivating. Allie was thrilled and proud that the show was such an immense success. The journey had been tortuous, but it had been worth it. If only she and Barry could sort out their relationship, all would be pretty much perfect.

Barry's postshow attentions were, however, centered on a different, less-complicated relationship.

"Keep the mask on. It's sexy," said Donna breathily as she lay back on his casino bed and opened her long, assistant legs invitingly in Barry's direction.

Barry's initial reaction to his bedroom encounter with Donna was understandably one of relief. He was relieved his sexual incapacity was apparently isolated to Allie alone. However, this feeling of elation was soon replaced by guilt and paranoia and a fervent desire to get the woman now snuggling under his left armpit out of his room as soon as possible.

"Jeez, it's after midnight," exclaimed Barry, twisting his left wrist so he could glance at his watch.

"Frightened I'll turn into a pumpkin, possum?" asked Donna.

"No, it's just that this was such a huge day and I should really get some sleep," Barry retorted.

"I'm tired too, dahlin'," yawned Donna, snuggling down farther. "Wake me up in time for breakfast."

Barry inwardly grimaced. He waited a moment and then tried another approach. "Here's the funny thing," he whispered. "I've never really been able to sleep with someone else in the bed."

Donna sat up. "You're throwing me out? You slept with me and now you're throwing me out?"

"No, of course not," Barry stammered. "I just meant I'm going to sleep on the sofa. The last thing I want is to disturb your night's sleep. You're . . . um . . . too important to me."

Barry slid out of the bed and tiptoed to the sofa. It was at this precise moment that Allie used the passkey Barry didn't know she possessed to enter the room armed with two glasses and the congratulatory bottle of vintage Dom Pérignon she had been given by a grateful casino. Barry, still wearing his mask, froze in the middle of the room. Donna was still sitting up in bed, her voluptuous breasts exposed and swaying slightly. It was hard to say who looked the most surprised—Barry, Donna, Allie, or the voluptuous breasts.

"Oh my God! Sorry!" said Allie, closing the door quickly.

"Shit!" Barry groaned as he collapsed onto the sofa.

Back in her room, Allie opened the champagne and wrapped herself around a large glass of it. Staring out at her suite's fabulous view of the Pacific, she considered the situation. She couldn't blame Donna for making a play for Barry, just as she couldn't blame Barry for attempting sex with someone else. Allie obviously repelled him, which was perfectly understandable. After all, she had been the one who had ended their marriage, and she had been the one whose actions had led to Barry's incarceration. There would be time enough in the future for Allie to find romance with someone. For now she needed to concentrate on hers and Barry's immensely promising business venture and her hidden, revenge-seeking agenda. The success of that had to be the number one priority. Indeed, maybe this was as good a time as any to reveal the complete truth to Barry about what Christian had done to them.

The next morning, Barry knocked gently on Allie's door. "Allie. Are you awake? Can we talk?"

"I'm not sure I can concentrate," she said, letting him in. "I'm still trying to get the disturbing mental image from last night out of my head."

"It didn't mean anything," Barry insisted.

Allie raised her hand. "Let me stop you right there. It's none of my business," she insisted. "We worked out professionally but not personally. I'm more than OK with that."

"But Allie . . . ," Barry pleaded.

"Let's not talk about it again. It's fine. Really," she said firmly. "Besides, I have something much more important to discuss with you."

"There's nothing more important to me than you," Barry said quietly.

"Oh, really?" said Allie. "You mean, you wouldn't like to know how Christian Sacco framed us and sent you to jail? And you wouldn't like to know how we could get him back for that?"

Barry sat down. An involuntary twitch at one corner of his mouth was the only indicator of his heightened emotional state.

"I'm listening," he said.

Allie pulled out the discs Jimmy Falanucci had given her and which she had been hiding in her jewelry box. They watched them in silence, and then Allie explained the whole counterfeiting scheme in detail to Barry.

"I don't understand what you're waiting for," said Barry. "Why haven't you taken this stuff to the cops and nailed his ass?"

"Because," said Allie. "I have something much more vindictive in mind."

Allie explained her whole, convoluted plan to Barry. He was impressed.

"So, what do you think?" she asked, after laying out every aspect of her scheme.

Barry leaned back in his chair and put his feet up on the ottoman in front of him.

"As I've told you before, you're the brains of this outfit," he said. "I guess I'll do whatever you suggest."

*Back in Las Vegas,* single-mother-of-two Brianna Murphy was taking giant steps up the corporate ladder. Her dominoes idea had worked phenomenally well. The first World Series of Dominoes was about to be staged at Heaven and already there were over three thousand participants signed up. Pamela Anderson had been contracted as the official spokesperson and a sizable five-year contract had been arranged with ESPN.

Christian transferred Brianna from Database Marketing to his old job of entertainment director. The casino was in the middle of building a new eighteen-hundred-seat theater for a Broadway show Christian had no confidence in. He'd recently made the mistake of going to New York to see the show rather than just reading the glowing East Coast reviews. The musical journey of a man romantically involved with his dog just wasn't going to fly in Vegas, even if it was set to the greatest hits of John Denver. He canceled the contract, kept building the theater, and gave Brianna the job of finding a replacement show to fill the new space.

Brianna had heard about a new show touting a masked magician that was doing a huge box office business at a casino in Australia. Brianna's interest had been further peaked by a recent article in *Variety,* which had confirmed the show's impressive numbers. Brianna knew magic had always done well in Las Vegas. This might be the very attraction Heaven needed. She resolved to fly down to Australia as soon as possible and check it out.

*The Mask had* been running for four months and every show had been a sellout. Allie and Barry should have been thrilled. However, Barry was itching to get back to Las Vegas to tackle Christian Sacco and was frustrated by Allie's insistence that they wait until she had all her metaphoric ducks in a row. Allie herself was concerned that she had yet to receive a reply from Heaven's new director of entertainment about the Mask show. Like Barry, despite whatever success they achieved, she felt her life would remain stuck in neutral until her plan to bring down Christian Sacco moved forward. So it was with immense relief that Allie received a call from Brianna Murphy's office confirming the casino executive's upcoming trip to Australia.

Barry and Allie decided to have a lunch together to celebrate the call and to commemorate their one-hundredth Australian performance. Coincidentally, that particular day was also Allie's twenty-ninth birthday. They went to one of their favorite restaurants that overlooked the ocean and feasted on lobster, scallops, sand crabs, and two bottles of a particularly fine Australian chardonnay.

"To us," Allie toasted.

"It's amazing what two people can achieve just by one going to jail and the other running a high-class call-girl operation," said Barry.

Allie giggled. "So what did you get me for my birthday?" she asked.

"I fired Donna."

Allie was surprised. "You didn't have to do that for me," she said.

"Yes, I did," said Barry. "For both of us."

"What about the hologram?" Allie inquired.

"I hired a new assistant who looks very similar," said Barry simply. "Just for the record, I only slept with her once."

"The new assistant?" asked Allie.

"Very funny," said Barry.

Barry knew Allie well enough to know that if their relationship was ever going to get back on track, he was going to have to make a grand gesture—grander than just firing Donna.

"I also bought you this," he announced.

Allie stared at the little black box Barry had placed on the table and was now pushing in her direction.

"Technically, of course, we're still, like, married," said Barry. "But I thought, given the circumstances, I should get you this."

Allie seemed dumbfounded.

"You asked me once what happened to me in prison," Barry said. "It's very simple. What happened to me was I realized how short a man's life is and how it can explode at any minute. You have to go for what you want when you want it."

"And you wanted to be a better magician and you are," said Allie, still not touching the box.

"The only reason I wanted to be a better magician was because I wanted you to love me again," admitted Barry.

"I always loved you, Barry," said Allie. "I always will. I don't need a ring to prove that."

"Good, 'cause there's nothing in the box."

"What?"

"Hey, I'm a magician. Empty boxes are my thing."

Allie grabbed the box and opened it. A flawless six-karat diamond engagement ring glinted in the sun.

"Damn," joked Barry. "Another trick that didn't work."

Allie had known for months that she had fallen completely in love with Barry all over again. She was desperate to renew the intimacy of their relationship, and this gesture told her he felt exactly the same way.

"Why don't we take the rest of this wine back to bed with us?" Allie suggested softly.

This time there wasn't a marshmallow or a piggy bank in sight.

# TWENTY

"Twelve people have died performing this trick," the Mask warned his audience.

A red light flickered around the mouth of the magician. It came from the laser-sighted gun that was pointed directly at Barry's head.

"Shoot!" the Mask ordered.

The finger of the audience member who had been

selected to help with the trick now squeezed the trigger and a loud explosion reverberated around the theater.

The Mask's head jerked back violently as he fell backward and hit the floor. A couple of people in the front section of the theater screamed.

Edie, the new assistant, ran onto the stage to tend to her fallen employer. As he stirred and got gingerly to his feet, the audience's enthusiastic applause increased in intensity as the Mask revealed that the bullet that had been previously autographed by the audience member/gunman was now clenched tightly between his teeth.

Nobody applauded more heartily than Brianna Murphy, sitting alone at the VIP table. She loved everything about the Mask's show, but had been particularly thrilled by the Indian rope trick, the flying Persian carpet, and the assistant decapitation. Now the Mask was coming into the audience and walking in her direction.

"Hello, beautiful young lady," whispered the Mask smoothly. "May I borrow your ring?"

"Will you give it back?" Brianna asked coyly.

"*I* would. My girlfriend, that's another story," he quipped.

Barry took the ring and moved on. He spotted another woman in the audience.

"Excuse me, miss, may I borrow your ring?"

"Certainly," the woman replied, prying it over her swollen knuckle.

"This is much easier than working for a living," Barry confided to the audience. "I'll just walk around and ask women for their rings."

The audience laughed.

"I need one more."

"Over here," a woman called out. "Take mine."

"Thank you very much, young lady," he replied, snatching the third ring. "It's at this point I would like to confess to you that I've been to prison."

The audience laughed again, this time a little nervously.

"But don't worry, not for robbery . . . only murder."

Barry placed the three rings in a large martini glass, slowly and one at a time.

"As you can see, these rings are entirely separate and want nothing to do with each other. Until, I swirl them around in the glass. Then . . ."

Barry shook the three rings back into the palm of his hand and held them up for the audience to see. They were now connected to each other and formed a chain.

"I'm not sure why this happens." The Mask's befuddled attitude added to his charm. He walked back over to Brianna and held the top ring up to her face.

"Is this your ring?"

"Yes," Brianna replied, amazed.

"Would you like two more?" Barry asked, handing her the three intertwined rings.

"Yes."

"Well, you can't have them," he chuckled, snatching them back. "They're mine."

The Mask placed them in the martini glass and swirled them around once again.

"Temporarily. My parole officer is in the audience tonight, so I'm going to have to give them back."

Laughter rippled through the crowd. The Mask once

again poured the three rings out of the glass and they tumbled out unconnected.

"Ladies and gentlemen, The Three-Rings-the-Magician-Has-to-Give-Back Trick," he proclaimed, throwing his arms up in the air in a grand, exclamatory gesture.

The audience exploded with laughter and applause as the Mask returned the three rings to their owners. Barry continued to be amazed at how well this trick was received. It was so simple. Although he collected three rings, only the first ring actually took part in the trick. He switched the second and third rings for two trick rings that could interconnect with the first legitimate ring. So when Brianna had examined the three rings, she had correctly identified the first as her own and assumed the other two belonged to the other two women who had donated jewelry. Incorrect assumption was a cornerstone of many tricks and scams, and the ring switch was a fine example of just how effectively it could work.

"I need a very specific volunteer for this final illusion," the Mask announced. "Who wants to go to the moon?"

Barry pointed to an older man toward the center of the audience. "You, sir. Would you join me up here?"

The man looked less than enthusiastic about becoming part of the Mask's show.

"You have an adventurous spirit, sir. I can feel it. Please come up here. You won't regret it," urged the Mask.

Bowing to the pressure, the man reluctantly stood up and made his way toward Barry. Edie, Barry's assistant, helped the man up onto the stage.

"What's your name?" Barry asked, extending his hand.

"Jim. Jim Jessop. From Caloundra," the man mumbled.

"Have you ever wanted to be an astronaut, Jim Jessop?" The audience giggled. Jim Jessop laughed. "No."

"Bring on the transporter ship," the Mask hollered to his staff.

With that, three black-clothed male assistants wheeled what looked like a rocket from a 1950s B movie onto the stage. Barry opened the front door to the apparatus, then paused. He turned and addressed the audience.

"We're not actually going to fly to the moon," explained the Mask. "That would take too long. This machine is going to break down our molecules and reconstitute them up there."

A murmur of skepticism traveled through the audience.

"You'll be able to see exactly what happens on that screen," the Mask advised, pointing to the large film screen that now descended from the theater's flies as he and his victim clambered into lightweight astrosuits.

"Just to make it interesting," the Mask continued, "I've asked my assistant Edie to pick up a few particular objects from the audience for us to take with us."

Edie now appeared on stage with a watch, a charm bracelet, and a coin purse.

"Whose purse?" the Mask continued.

"Mine," a woman said from the back of the room.

"Have we ever met before?"

"Never."

"Whose charm bracelet?"

"That's mine," Brianna shouted out.

As per her preshow orders from Allie, Edie had been sure to take something of Brianna's.

"Very pretty. Asian, yes?"

"From Thailand," Brianna answered.

"And the watch?"

"That's mine. And I want it back," said a male voice from the left side of the auditorium.

The audience and the Mask laughed good-naturedly.

The Mask placed the three objects in a black velvet bag.

"Are you ready for our moon trip, Jim?" the Mask asked.

"I guess so," said a slightly bemused Jim Jessop.

"Then off we go."

The Mask bundled his victim and himself into the machine and closed the entrance. There was a flash of light and Edie pulled the door back open. The Mask and Jim Jessop had both disappeared.

The lights on the stage dimmed as an image on the projector screen began to flicker into life. It showed the surface of the moon. Gradually, the Mask and Jim Jessop began to rematerialize, the magician holding the black velvet bag.

The Mask addressed the camera. "Well, here we are," he said simply. "How are you back on the Gold Coast?"

Brianna sat puzzled. Obviously, since instantaneous planetary travel wasn't possible, the film had to have been pretaped and the audience member had to be a plant. But what if her bracelet really was in that bag?

"Just to prove to you that this is real," continued the Mask, "have a look at this."

The magician knelt down in the moondust and began to open the velvet bag.

The camera cut to a close-up of the bag as the Mask pulled out its contents; the coin purse, the watch, and

Brianna's charm bracelet were now somehow on the moon. Now that *was* impressive.

The Mask replaced the three items in the bag, and the camera pulled back to reveal Jim and the Mask now bouncing weightlessly around the moon's surface, the velvet bag held tightly in the magician's fist at all times. The Mask grabbed a handful of dust from the moon's surface just as both men began to evaporate. Onstage, moments later, Edie pulled open the door to the rocket and the two men got out.

The audience jumped to its feet and applauded as the Mask poured moondust onto the stage and then returned the items to the three audience members. He leaned into Brianna and whispered into her ear so she could hear him above the roaring rock music that signaled the end of the show was imminent: "Come backstage. We'll talk."

The flying Persian carpet had been repositioned. The Mask got on it, waved good-bye to his adoring audience, and flew into the air and off the stage. The houselights came up and the emotionally exhausted audience took a collective breath, and then began to buzz about how wonderful the show had been.

Brianna suddenly noticed that Allie had appeared at her shoulder.

"Follow me," Allie ordered.

*The interior designer* of Barry's dressing room had chosen the Rat Pack as thematic inspiration, and so a large mural of Sammy, Frank, and Dean occupied one wall while the room's furniture and fittings included a lot of black leather, gold accenting, and cocktail paraphernalia. Barry had already slipped on a cotton monogrammed bathrobe and was preparing a cup of tea with lemon, his favorite after-show concoction.

"Do you mind if I take this off?" Barry asked Brianna, removing his mask.

He was handsome, Brianna noticed. He was also not Lord Lucan, Prince Harry, Bill Clinton's younger brother, or Elvis Presley. These were all possible Mask identities the local media had guessed at over the past couple of months.

"I loved the show," said Brianna. "I thought it was brilliant."

"Thank you," said Barry. "It's really a joint effort between Allie and me."

"Well, congratulations. I really want to get you guys to come to Heaven."

Allie allowed herself a small smile of triumph. "I've heard great things about that casino," she said. "It's supposed to be beautiful."

"It is," said Brianna, looking over the notes she had made during the show. "There are three other people in your show, yes? Two male assistants and one female?"

Barry and Allie both laughed. "There are thirty-eight other people in the show, Brianna," Allie confided.

At that moment, the door swung open and Jim Jessop from Caloundra entered the room.

"Just wanted to say g'day before I left," he announced. "See you next Thursday, right?"

"Right," confirmed Allie.

Even though she now knew for sure that Jim was a

plant, Brianna was still baffled as to how the Mask's final trick had been accomplished. However, she had a feeling that the pit of fake moondust and the cameraman she had passed on her journey back to the dressing room had something to do with it.

"I should get ready for the next show," Barry said to Allie. "Why don't you two ladies sort out all the details over dinner?"

He turned to Brianna. "I leave all the business decisions to Allie. We're a team," he told her.

"All good marriages are," said Brianna.

She noticed the look that passed between Allie and Barry.

"Sorry, did I get that wrong? You are married, yes?"

Allie snuck her arm around Barry's waist. "Yes, we are," she said.

# TWENTY-ONE

Christian Sacco was too busy to attend the first two performances of the Mask's show. He was hearing great things about this new magician, though, and was quick to phone anyone who mattered and claim responsibility.

"Hi, Richard," he said into his office speakerphone as he fed the fish in his table.

"Hi, Christian. What's up?" said Richard Summerford irritably.

Summerford disliked being talked to on a speaker-phone; it indicated that the caller did not consider the person on the other end important enough for the caller to speak into the receiver. Richard immediately pushed the speaker button on his own phone and slid his chair a couple of feet back to counter Christian's disrespect.

"I wanted to invite you and the other members of the board to see my new show tonight," said Christian smugly. "It's tremendous."

Richard had just read a rave about the show in that morning's local paper.

"For you, Christian, anything," he replied smoothly.

"What?" asked Christian, unable to hear what Richard was saying.

Richard repeated his intention slightly louder. Christian still wasn't sure of Richard's response but decided his tone of voice veered toward the positive.

"As always, Richard, I really appreciate your support," replied Christian unctuously.

Christian was unsure whether or not to bring a date to the Mask's show. Of late, he had been dating hookers exclusively. However, people might consider it odd if he didn't bring a companion. In the end, he decided to phone his favorite call girl and invite her to attend as his prop date. Ironically, he had tried to date Angela Porter when she had worked at Heaven and she had always turned him down. A few months into his tenure as president,

Security had alerted Christian to the fact that Angela was trying to pick up customers in Cosmos, and as president of the casino he felt obligated to punish her in the privacy of his own office. He had been paying to see her off and on ever since.

Life had not gone particularly well for Angela since Allie had left the look-alike hooker business solely in her charge. Angela had screwed up the operation by greedily charging too much money, cutting down on security, and not fostering new talent. Gradually all of her best girls had drifted away, and eventually Angela concluded it made more sense to return to working as an individual. However, she was on the wrong side of thirty-five, the late nights were beginning to catch up with her, and along the way she had managed to pick up an expensive cocaine habit. She now had four or five regular customers, of which Christian was the best, and she was struggling to pay her overpriced rent each month. Seeing a show sounded like fun to her, and little in her life was fun these days. She just hoped that afterward, Christian wouldn't insist on tying her to that damn fish table.

After a couple of toots of the premium coke she had been assured by her dealer had not been stepped on since beginning its journey north from Colombia, Angela met Christian for a preshow drink in Cosmos, and together they made their way toward the theater for the eight o'clock performance of the new magic sensation from Australia.

"I think the mask thing is kinda hot," admitted Angela as they admired the giant photograph of the Mask displayed above the box office.

"I'll wear one later," said Christian, giving Angela's rump a squeeze. "Maybe I'll get the fish to wear masks, too."

Angela smiled wanly, realizing the fish table was once again in her future.

"Does he look familiar to you?" asked Christian, studying the Mask's likeness.

"Only from the newspaper ads," said Angela.

There was something about the performer that reminded Christian of someone, but he could recall neither the person nor the context. Just then, Richard Summerford tapped him on the shoulder.

"Congratulations, Christian," he said. "Big hit."

"Thanks."

"Hello, Angela," continued Richard, kissing his ex-employee on the cheek. "I haven't seen you forever."

"Not since you fired me," replied Angela.

"Nothing personal. You always did a great job for us," said Richard quickly, smiling his widest smile. "See you after the show, Christian."

*Allie stayed hidden* backstage until after the show began, then snuck into the back of the auditorium to watch her plan unfold. As ever, the Mask's show was proceeding flawlessly and the illusions were all being appreciated by a particularly attentive audience.

"May I have the houselights up, please. I need a very specific volunteer for this final illusion," the Mask announced. "I want somebody who really thinks he needs to get away from it all."

In the wings, Barry's two main assistants, who were

preparing to wheel on the rocket apparatus, suddenly appeared concerned.

"He's never said that before," commented the first assistant.

"We'd better concentrate if he's going off script," warned his associate.

"Wow! There's somebody in this audience with a really powerful aura," said the Mask. "It's the gentleman over here. You, sir."

The Mask's hand shot out and pointed right at Christian. "Will you come up here, please?" the Mask commanded.

Christian demurred, but the Mask stood his ground. People around Christian began to encourage him, especially Richard Summerford, who was enjoying Christian's discomfort.

"Go on, Christian," whispered Angela. "Get it over with."

The personification of reluctance, Christian was helped up onto the stage by Edie. At the back of the auditorium, Allie felt her heartbeat quicken.

"What's your name?" she heard Barry ask.

"Christian Sacco," said Christian. "I run this casino."

"Really? Then I'd better not make a mistake, huh?" retorted the Mask.

"No, you'd better not," said Christian humorlessly.

"Have you ever done something you feel really, really guilty about?"

Christian shrugged. "Not particularly."

In the wings, the two assistants exchanged glances. Where was Barry going with this? He had completely abandoned the script, and they wondered how the rocket prop could work using a real audience member rather than a plant.

"I want you to humor me and try a little experiment," said the Mask. "Stare forward into the audience and let your mind go blank."

Christian reluctantly did as he was told.

"I am going to try to dig in your memory and find the event I am feeling. Hold my hands and I'll attempt to get something about that event to appear on the screen above us."

Allie was by now in the sound and lighting booth directing the technicians, who were completely lost by what was occurring on stage. "Lower the projector screen," she ordered. The projector screen usually used in the moonwalk trick began to descend.

"Concentrate, Christian. Let's see what we can find," said the Mask, standing behind his victim and holding both of Christian's hands tightly.

"Run VT," ordered Allie.

The special videotape the technicians had been supplied with by Allie just prior to the show now began to play.

"Hello," said Allie's image. "My name is Allie Bowen. The audience member now standing on the stage used to be my boyfriend. I guess he stopped being my boyfriend when he framed me for a crime I didn't commit. Let me tell you the story of what exactly happened."

The color drained from Christian's face and he unsuccessfully tried to wriggle his arm free from Barry's powerful grip. He stood powerless to do anything but listen to

Allie's voice explain in horrifying detail exactly how he had once swindled the casino he now ran and how he had laid the blame on two entirely innocent people.

"I don't expect you to simply believe my version of events," Allie's prerecorded monologue continued. "I have evidence. Here's a recording of when Christian Sacco first asked this casino's head of security, a man named Jimmy Falanucci, whom Christian was blackmailing, to plant counterfeiting equipment in a garage behind Industrial Road."

The image now switched to a close-up of Christian.

"What can I do for you, Christian?" said Jimmy Falanucci offscreen.

"I need a favor," said Christian.

"I want to do you one."

"Excellent. Give us a moment, Brooke."

A topless woman crossed the frame. A few men in the confused audience cheered.

"I need some machinery being freighted in from LA to be picked up at the airport and taken to a garage. Quickly and quietly."

"That it?"

The next part was the part that always made Allie's stomach knot. She couldn't believe she had once loved a man who could be this destructive.

"It's a surprise delivery; the garage is going to be locked. I need someone who can get in and out without leaving any footprints. Know anyone who can do that?"

"Sure. Me."

"Thanks, Jimmy."

The screen went blank. In the lighting booth, Allie held

her breath. She hoped Richard Summerford was beginning to realize just how badly he'd been duped.

"What is this bullshit?" said Christian unconvincingly.

"Wait," said the Mask cheerfully as he tightened his grasp on Christian. "This next bit's even better."

"Christian Sacco gave me an envelope full of counterfeit chips and then lied about it," Allie now announced from the screen. "Here's the piece of surveillance video he made Jimmy Falanucci remove. It would have exonerated me and confirmed his guilt."

The audience watched the footage of Christian and Allie in Pandora's Lunchbox and saw Christian clearly hand her an envelope. In the fifth row, Richard Summerford began to seethe.

"Christian didn't know Jimmy Falanucci taped my office that day with a concealed camera," the on-screen Allie told the audience. "I didn't know. Until Jimmy gave me this footage a few weeks before he died."

Black-and-white footage of Christian Sacco blatantly planting the chips behind Allie's bookcase was the final outrage for Summerford. He fumbled for his cell phone and called for Security.

The screen went black. The audience was puzzled. This final trick wasn't anything like as good as the rest of the Mask's show. They waited to see what would happen next. Just then a man stood up in the auditorium and pointed at Christian Sacco.

"Security," Richard Summerford barked at the guards who had just arrived, "detain that man!"

Barry was happy to hand a struggling Christian over to

the gaggle of armed St. Peters that appeared on stage moments later.

At the back of the theater, Allie emerged from the technical booth and approached a camera crew snuggled uncomfortably against the back wall.

"Did you get all that?" Allie asked Rikki Green, the local NBC reporter whom she had invited to the show with the lure of seeing something really special. Rikki's cameraman was busy getting shots or the struggling Christian Sacco being dragged up the aisle of the theater.

"It'll be on the eleven o'clock broadcast," promised Rikki. "Thanks for the exclusive."

Allie put herself in the path of Christian and his captors.

"Hi, Christian, remember me?" she asked.

Christian's mouth dangled open in shock.

"And remember Barry?"

Christian turned and looked back at the stage. Barry had removed his mask and Christian realized he was staring at the man he had unjustly sent to prison.

Allie leaned into Christian and repeated the words he had once spat into her ear. "Did you honestly think I'd let you treat me like that? Do you know anything about me at all?"

"Fuck you, Allie," he spat. "I made you. I taught you, you uptight bitch. How dare you do this to me? I will make you suffer. I'm Christian Sacco."

"Not anymore you're not," said Richard Summerford icily, appearing at Allie's side.

"I'll tell people about Bangkok," said Christian desperately to Summerford. "I'll tell your wife."

"We divorced two months ago," said Richard matter-of-factly. "Very quietly and very amicably."

For the first time, Christian visibly sagged. He had no cards left. He had no life left.

Allie felt an immense surge of relief. It was over. Justice had been done. The balance of her universe had been corrected. She inhaled and exhaled deeply, feeling as though it was the first real breath she had taken since this whole horror had engulfed her. The entire experience had been a terrifying journey, but the important truth was that it had left her and Barry in a far better place than the one in which they had began.

"Bye, Christian," said Allie, indicating to the guards that they should continue on their way. "Be sure not to write."

*Allie's plan had* worked perfectly. Christian Sacco was headed for jail and Barry was exonerated. A bonus effect Allie had not foreseen was Richard Summerford arranging for Brianna Murphy to succeed Christian, thereby ordaining the first female president of a Strip casino. Brianna arranged with Allie to extend Barry's multimillion-dollar deal for a further five years, allowing him to continue to dazzle enthusiastic Vegas visitors. Separately, Richard Summerford also approved an unspecified large settlement for damages paid by Heaven to Barry Morris, aka Barry Houdini, aka the Mask.

Barry and Allie pulled off their best trick a few months later when she discovered that she was pregnant.

"Do you want a boy or a girl?" asked Allie as they sat contentedly on the balcony of their newly purchased Tournament Place penthouse, which overlooked the Strip.

"Either would be wonderful, babe," admitted Barry. "Just so long as it isn't a rabbit."

# Harrah's across America
## See Rita Rudner live at Harrah's in Las Vegas.

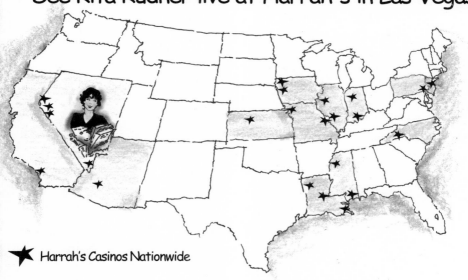

★ Harrah's Casinos Nationwide

Harrah's Phoenix Ak-Chin Casino
Harrah's Rincon San DiegoCasino
Harrah's Joliet Casino
Harrah's Metropolis Casino
Caesars Indiana
Horseshoe Casino Hammond
Harrah's Council Bluffs Casino
Horseshoe Council Bluffs
Harrah's Prairie Band Casino
Harrah's Louisiana Downs
Harrah's Lake Charles Casino
Harrah's New Orleans Casino
Horseshoe Casino Bossier City
Grand Casino Biloxi
Grand Casino Gulfport
Grand Casino Tunica
Horseshoe Casino Tunica
Sheraton Casino & Hotel Tunica
Harrah's North Kansas City

Harrah's St. Louis Casino
Bally's Las Vegas
Bill's Casino Lake Tahoe
Caesars Palace
Flamingo Las Vegas
Harrah's Lake Tahoe Casino
Harrah's Las Vegas Casino
Harrah's Laughlin Casino
Harrah's Reno Casino
Harveys Lake Tahoe Casino
Paris Las Vegas
Rio All-Suite Hotel & Casino
Bally's Atlantic City
Caesars Atlantic City
Harrah's Atlantic City Casino
Showboat Casino
Harrah's Cherokee Casino
Harrah's Chester